Also by John Wilson

WINGS
OF WAR

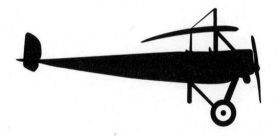

JOHN WILSON

DOUBLEDAY CANADA

Library and Archives Canada Cataloguing in Publication

Wilson, John (John Alexander), 1951-, author
Wings of war / John Wilson.

ISBN 978-0-385-67830-8

eBook ISBN 978-0-385-67831-5
(epub)

I. Title.

PS8595.I5834W56 2014   jC813'.54   C2013-906366-8
C2013-906367-6

Issued in print and electronic formats.

Cover image: Heritage Image Partnership / Alamy
Cover design: Rachel Cooper
Printed and bound in the USA

Published in Canada by Doubleday Canada,
a division of Random House of Canada Limited,
a Penguin Random House Company
www.randomhouse.ca

10 9 8 7 6 5 4 3 2 1

Dedicated to the memory of Lanoe Hawker, VC, DSO,
the first British flying ace and, on 23 November 1916,
the Red Baron's eleventh victim.

CHAPTER 1

Dreams of Freedom—July 1914

The snap of the high-tension wire giving way echoes like a gunshot over the flat prairie field. Abby, the chestnut mare I've ridden over from my folks' place, twitches her ears and looks up. Above her an extraordinary contraption of wood, fabric and wire wobbles dangerously. I see where the wire's gone— it's about halfway along the right wings. Both twist oddly, and my uncle Horst, crouching on the old tractor seat in the middle of the plane, wrestles with the controls, fighting to find a balance between too much speed, which will rip the weakened wings off, and too little, which will stall the flight. Either way the plane will plummet to the ground—certain death for my uncle from over seventy feet up.

I hold my breath and clench my fists as I watch. The rough coughing sound of the engine comes and goes as the machine bucks and turns. The plane clears the trees around the farmhouse and sinks slowly toward the stubble field beside the barn. Horst is winning his battle for control! I let my breath out as the large baby-carriage wheels touch down. Almost immediately, the contraption lurches to the right, the lower wing tip touches the ground and, with a loud snapping sound, the wings fold up like crumpled paper. The engine races wildly and the propeller shatters, sending knife-like pieces of wood slashing through the air.

I vault the fence and run to the wreck. By the time I arrive, my uncle is hauling himself out of the mass of broken wood, torn fabric and twisted wires. His jacket has a long rip in the sleeve, and there's already a swelling bruise on his forehead. He says something in German, and from his tone of voice, I'm glad I can't understand him.

"Uncle Horst!" I shout. "Are you okay?"

"Ya, ya, Edward," my uncle says, brushing himself down and gazing mournfully at the ruins of his prized flying machine. "But Bertha, she is kaput."

My uncle calls every flying machine he builds

Bertha. As close as I can figure, the pile of wreckage in front of me is *Bertha 6*.

"She was a beauty," Horst says, bending to lift the tip of one of his hand-carved wooden propeller blades from where it has embedded itself in the ground. "But too heavy. The two wings, they do not give enough lift."

"Why not add a third wing?" I suggest. "I read in the newspapers that they have those over in Europe. Triplanes, I think they're called."

"Ya, ya. Another wing. Another wing. Another wing. Biplanes. Triplanes. With each wing I get more lift, but more weight also. And I have only twenty-five horses." Horst aims a kick at the bulky engine that lies beside Bertha, crackling as it cools.

"Can't you get a bigger engine?"

"Oh, ya. I will get one hundred horses and build a machine that will fly to Moose Jaw. But I buy this magnificent engine with what? You might as well say, 'Uncle Horst, buy an aeroplane.' I would work this farm for twenty years to save enough dollars to buy one of the Wright boys' Flyers or a Blériot."

"Blériot?" I ask. "Wasn't he the famous pilot who was the first to fly across the English Channel?"

"Ya. Five years past. But, Edward, this is 1914. The world has moved on and still he sells the same plane. What use will old planes be in the war that is coming?"

"War? What war?"

"Do you not read the newspapers?"

"Of course I read the newspapers," I say indignantly. "The only war they talk about is the trouble in Ireland. What does that have to do with Blériot's flying machines?"

"You read the papers of the English. They are blind. They look only in their own backyard and their empire. They do not look at Europe. You should read the German newspapers."

"I don't read German. You know that."

My uncle ignores my protests. "That man who was shot last month with his wife—"

"Archduke Franz Ferdinand," I interrupt, eager to show Horst that I *do* know something about Europe. "He was assassinated in some place I've never heard of."

"Sarajevo," Horst says. "It is in the Balkans."

"Yeah," I say, "but the Balkans are a long way off, and besides, they're always having wars down there. The assassination was almost a month ago, and nothing's happened since then."

"Much has happened, which you would know if you read the correct newspapers." Horst waves the fragment of propeller to silence me. "And do not dismiss a place simply because you have never heard of it. Anyway, it is not this place that is important—it is the person. The man who shot the archduke is a Serbian, and Austria would very much like to make Serbia part of her empire. There has already been some shooting along the border."

"But there was a war in the Balkans last year. It didn't affect us."

Horst stares at the ground and sighs. "This time it may be different."

"What do you mean?"

"The Russian bear is watching. She will help Serbia, and Kaiser Wilhelm will go to war to help Austria. Even France will be drawn into the insanity. Germany will be fighting two wars, front and back, east and west. All of Europe will be in flames."

I stare at Horst, shocked by what he is suggesting. There has been no European war since Napoleon was defeated almost a hundred years ago. "It won't happen," I say. "And even if you're right, this war won't affect England and Canada."

"Ya. Of course you are right, Edward." Horst takes a deep breath and smiles. "It won't affect us all the way out here in Saskatchewan. It is just one more squabble between those crazy Europeans."

"Would flying machines be used in a war?" I ask, unable to shake the thought of marching armies.

"Flying machines should make us poor earth-bound humans free—like the birds. They should not be used

THE INSPIRATION FOR BERTHA.

for war and killing." Horst looks at me, his pale blue eyes intense. "But ya, I think flying machines will be used. From up there"—he thrusts his arm straight up toward the sky—"one man will be able to see what an entire army is doing. There will be no secrets anymore. And some men—your English writer H.G. Wells for one—think that one day there will be great battles among the clouds, as well as flying machines that can carry bombs big enough to destroy whole cities." Horst lowers his arm and turns his head to survey his farm. "But we are safe here. Who would wish to waste bombs on my poor fields?

"You would like to fly?" he asks, surprising me with his abrupt change of topic.

"I'd love to," I say eagerly.

"Then I shall put two seats in my next Bertha. I will take you up. We will soar like the birds and laugh at the poor people on the ground below."

"Will you?" My heart races at the mere thought of being up there with the birds, looking down.

"I promise," Horst says with a smile. "But first I must rebuild." My uncle stares down at *Bertha 6*'s remains. "Perhaps two wings is my mistake," he muses quietly. "Maybe one wing—a monoplane—would be enough if it is designed correctly." He fumbles in his overall pockets for a greasy notebook and the stub of a pencil. "And I know a man in Moose Jaw who says he might be able to get me a bigger engine, maybe fifty horses. It will need work, but . . ." Horst finds an empty page in his notebook and begins scribbling figures across it. His mumbled conversation with himself reverts to German.

I've seen this happen before. He'll be lost to the world until he's worked out whatever's on his mind. If he doesn't get the answer he seeks, he'll still be standing in the middle of his field when it is too dark to see the page in his hand.

"I have to get back," I say. "I have chores to do. The chickens need feeding, and Dad wants me to clean out the stalls in the barn. He says now that I'm not going to school, I should be doing more work around the farm."

Horst grunts at me and waves his hand vaguely. Staring at the sky, I walk over to Abby. Will my uncle build a flying machine that can take me up as well? What'll it be like up there, diving and swooping hundreds of feet above the ground? What will the world look like? Will I be free?

I ride Abby the four miles home at a walk, wondering, dreaming and questioning. The late afternoon sky is clear, with only a few puffy white clouds hugging the horizon. It's endless and so much more interesting than the flat land that stretches away from me on all sides. I focus on a red-tailed hawk far above, his broad wings motionless as he soars effortlessly in lazy circles. How far can he see? He owns the world. Of course, he doesn't need a heavy, smelly engine thumping and roaring away to keep him up there, but that's a price I would gladly pay to fly. "I hope Horst can build an aeroplane that can take me up there," I say to Abby, who waggles her ears in response.

Uncle Horst came over to Canada as a child, more than forty years ago. His father was a button-maker in Berlin, Ontario. I guess making buttons didn't seem that exciting to Horst, so he drifted out west, bought a quarter-section farm, married my dad's sister, Martha, and settled down. Well, his body settled down, but his mind never did. He loves machinery and is always the first in the county to buy the latest farming gadget—Mr. Ford's gasoline-powered tractor, a new automatic milking machine or a reaper with a knotting binder.

My dad often tells Horst that he is the worst farmer west of Winnipeg, spending all his time tinkering with some new idea for a flying machine instead of filling his barn with bales of hay. Uncle Horst just laughs and says, "Ya, but I build the best flying machines!" Dad says Uncle Horst would have starved to death if he hadn't married Aunt Martha to run the farm for him.

The first Bertha I met was number 3. That was in the summer of 1910, when I was twelve years old and nagging Dad to let me leave school to work on the farm. *Bertha 3* was a strange complex of wings, struts, wires and an odd box-like tail. She flew quite well, but not well enough for Horst. *Bertha 3* didn't survive the winter; she was dismantled and rebuilt as *Bertha 4*. Unfortunately, something in number 4's wings didn't work, and she had a short and unhappy life. *Bertha 5* worked better and flew around the farm scaring the animals throughout 1912.

It took Horst most of 1913 to develop and build *Bertha 6*, which is why the crash I just witnessed is such a blow. Still, I have left my uncle with pencil and notebook in hand, and I am certain that *Bertha 7* is already growing in his mind, rising like a phoenix from the wreckage of her predecessor. I sat in *Bertha 6* and even drove her around the field, but I have never left the ground. That is my dream.

In my daydream I'm up there with the hawk. I can see the railway line stretching off to the east and west, the grain elevators of Mortlach and Parkbeg rising up to break the monotony. The wheat fields are a patchwork quilt below me, and the occasional cows mere toys. There's Old Man Dudek driving his buggy into town to sell eggs and pierogies. I feel as if I could reach down and pick him up. That would surprise him! I could even drop a bag of flour on him for a joke. Or a bomb.

My daydream becomes darker and I imagine armies marching back and forth across the fields—long, curving lines of men in red and blue uniforms snaking toward one another. Cavalry troops, their helmets and breastplates gleaming in the sun, sweep out in front, probing for the enemy. Cannons are unlimbered, and puffs of dark smoke rise from their muzzles. Shells explode bloodily among the soldiers. I can almost hear the thunder of the explosions, the crack of the rifles and the screams of the wounded. Is this what it would be like? Is this what aeroplanes are going to be used for?

My daydream is horrifying, but it's exciting as well. After all, I'm not down there with the soldiers or the cavalry, marching, fighting, dying. I'm far up above in the clean air, free, safe, detached. "If Canada ever goes to war," I say to Abby, "I'm going to become a pilot. No marching and fighting for me!" Ignoring me, Abby continues her steady plodding pace toward home, a brush-down and a tub of oats.

CHAPTER 2

Shadows of War—August 1914

WAR IS DECLARED.

"Well, Horst, your predictions of war were correct," my dad says. It's August 6, 1914, and Canada declared war on Germany yesterday.

Horst and Martha have come over for dinner. Mom and Martha are gossiping in the kitchen, while Dad, Horst and I sit on the porch watching the sky turn blood red as the sun touches the far horizon. Dad and Horst nurse glasses of brandy. I have a glass as well, but even though my sixteenth birthday is mere weeks away, my brandy is heavily watered down. If I'm honest, I'm glad of the dilution. The harsh taste stings my throat, and I only demanded some so I wouldn't feel left out.

"Ya," Horst agrees, "but I was wrong about England. I thought she would sit to one side and watch. And now Canada is at war as well." My uncle stares glumly into his glass.

"We couldn't just let the German army march through Belgium," Dad says. "Someone has to protect the small countries."

Horst regards his drink for a moment longer. "I do not think it is just about Belgium," he says eventually. "The German papers say that England is jealous of Germany's navy and does not want competition for her empire."

"Is that what you think, Horst?" Dad asks.

Horst smiles. "I have not talked with Kaiser Wilhelm recently. All I know for sure is that the world is much more complicated than the newspapers—English or German—tell us."

"Indeed," Dad agrees. "I'm grateful for a simple life

on the farm. Speaking of which, it will be a good harvest this fall if the weather holds."

"And if enough young men stay behind to bring the crop in," Horst adds.

Dad nods. "The French say they will be in Berlin by Christmas."

"And the Germans say they will be in Paris by the same time," Horst counters. "I think they are both wrong." My dad opens his mouth to say something, but Horst stands and raises a hand to stop him. "Enough talk of war," he says. "I must return to my simple farm. Thank you for a most pleasant evening, and let us hope the next time it will be in happier circumstances. Edward, would you be kind enough to inform Martha that I am readying the wagon?"

"Of course," I say.

Amid more expressions of hope for better times, we say our goodbyes, and Horst and Martha disappear into the gathering dark.

Dad and I settle back on the porch as moths bang stupidly against the gas lantern and mosquitoes begin to discover us.

"Will all the young men really go off and fight in the war?" I ask.

"I'm afraid so," Dad says. "They say there are lines at the recruiting offices in Toronto and Regina already."

"But there won't be time for them to get over to Europe before the war ends."

Dad takes a sip of his brandy. "I'm not so sure. I suspect that this war's not going to be like the ones you read about in books. It's not going to be a thin line of British redcoats standing against a horde of poorly armed natives in some forgotten corner of the empire. It won't even be the big battles that Napoleon or Wellington would recognize. The world has changed. France, Germany and Russia have millions of men on the march, and they have weapons that Napoleon could only dream of."

"So the war will last into next year?"

"And then some. The war the Americans fought against themselves lasted four years, and this is a much bigger affair than that." Dad tilts his head, furrows his brow and stares hard at me. "This war might even last long enough for you to be old enough to join up."

I haven't thought about this until now. I've been interested in what is happening in Europe—excited, even—but it is a distant place and doesn't seem to have much to do with our little corner of the prairies. Will I join up when I'm old enough?

"Uncle Horst says that aeroplanes will be important in this war."

"He may be right. New things are always tried out

in wars." Dad looks at me questioningly. "What are you thinking?"

"I'm not sure. The war seems a long way off, but Canada's in it now. If it goes on for a long time, I'll have to do my part, but I don't know if I want to be a soldier—at least not one in an army of millions. If Uncle Horst teaches me to fly, then I can be a pilot." The instant I say it, I know it's what I want to do. I'm thrilled by the idea of being far above the fighting, like an ancient Greek god staring down on mere mortals from Mount Olympus.

"That might be a good idea," Dad says, nodding. "I don't expect a soldier's lot will be much fun in this war." He stands up and stretches. "Meanwhile, let's hope the papers are right and this madness is all over soon. I'm heading inside before the mosquitoes drain all the blood out of me. Goodnight, Edward."

"Goodnight, Dad."

Despite the mosquitoes, I sit on the porch for a bit longer, staring into the darkness. The stars are out—the same stars that the millions of soldiers mobilizing all across Europe can see. I feel excited to be alive to see these momentous events unfold, but if I'm honest with myself, I feel scared as well. Will this war get so big that I'll be sucked in to become just another soldier? Not if I can help it. I resolve that as soon as possible, I'll ride over and persuade Uncle Horst to teach me to fly. In exchange, I'll offer to help him build *Bertha 7*. Even if the war ends before I'm old enough to enlist, I'll still have fulfilled my dream of rising in the air to soar with the birds.

CHAPTER 3

Escaping Gravity—June 1915

"You must concentrate," Horst tells me. "If you break your neck, your father will be angered at me." I am sitting in *Bertha 7* at one end of Horst's field. The building, the testing, the adjusting, the practicing— all these are over. I'm sixteen, and I'm about to fly an aeroplane on my own for the first time.

My heart is thumping like a steam hammer. I'm scared and excited at the same time. The multitude of wires holding Bertha together make me feel as if I'm in the center of a web, but am I the spider or the fly? Am I in control or am I trapped?

"Remember your axes, Edward," Horst says seriously, forcing me to concentrate. "You have three of them going through you—one up and down, one side to side, and one forward and back. Forget left and right. You control only the spin of yourself and the plane around each of those three axes. You are not the *pilot* of the plane—you are *part* of the plane. I have told you this many times. Imagine the axes are running through your body, head to toe, elbow to elbow, spine to belly button. What is rotation around the head-to-toe axis called?"

"Yaw," I reply.

"And the elbow-to-elbow axis?"

"Pitch."

"And spine to belly button?"

"Roll. I know all this, Horst," I say in exasperation.

"Ya, ya, you know. But you must *remember*."

"I've been up a dozen times."

"Only twelve, and I was with you to stop your mistakes. This time I will not be there to get you out of trouble. And Bertha, she will be different without me—lighter, faster."

The past ten months have been hectic. Every moment that Dad has been able to spare me from the farm, I've been Horst's dogsbody, holding, carving, gluing pieces of wood, stretching control wires and lifting heavy engines. I have countless scars and bruises, and an annoying cough from hours spent inhaling the foul fumes given off by the glue that holds Bertha together and the liquid—dope, Horst calls it—that is used to cure the fabric of the wings. But every moment has been worth it. *Bertha 7* is finished and she is beautiful.

At shoulder height, a single wing stretches away on either side of me. A profusion of wires support the wings, splaying out like a parasol from the pole rising in front of me. The wings themselves and the fuselage I sit in are covered in doped fabric, but behind me, stretching away to the covered tail, is an open mesh of struts. Out of sight below me are more struts, to which are fixed four wheels from an old baby carriage. Wires run from these struts to help support the wings. In front of me, and blocking most of my view as Bertha sits on the ground, is the massive fifty-horsepower, six-cylinder engine that Horst acquired cheaply from his contact in Moose Jaw. In front of that stands my uncle, lecturing me and grasping one of the two vast propeller blades.

"Check the controls." Horst's stern instructions interrupt my thoughts. "Yaw."

I look down to where my feet rest on a solid wooden bar. I push down my right foot and look over my shoulder to see the rudder on the vertical tailfin move to the right. In the air this will make me swing to the right, or rotate around the up-and-down axis. I repeat the process with my left foot and give Horst the thumbs-up.

"Pitch," he shouts.

I grasp the control stick rising from the floor between my knees and pull it toward me. I look back and see the flaps on the horizontal tail surfaces rise. This will make me climb, or rotate around the side-to-side axis. I push the stick away and imagine myself diving. I give the thumbs-up.

"Roll."

I move the control stick to the right and check that the flaps on the wings—Horst calls them ailerons—move up on the right side and down on the left. This will cause Bertha to roll to the right in flight, or rotate around the front-to-back axis. I repeat the movement to the left and wave a thumb forward.

Apart from the engine throttle, which is screwed onto a wooden spar in front of me and controls the flow of fuel to the engine, these are the only controls. It's simple, but it's hard to remember everything in the air, and moving in three dimensions is much more difficult than directing Abby left, right, forward or back on solid ground.

"Contact!" Horst yells.

I pull the throttle out a little and give him the thumbs-up.

My uncle hesitates and looks at me. "Be careful," he says.

I nod.

Horst throws all his weight on the propeller blade and dives to one side. The engine coughs and a puff of dark smoke spits out of the exhaust. The propeller kicks round. I pull the throttle out a little more. The coughs come closer together and the propeller speeds up. More throttle. The coughs unite into a deep, shuddering roar and the propeller blurs. Bertha jerks forward, eager to be off. More throttle. The engine sound smooths and Bertha speeds up.

I'm clenching the control stick so tightly that the knuckles on my left hand are white. I have to concentrate on not moving the stick left or right. If I do, Bertha will roll, the wing will catch the ground, she'll be wrecked, and if I survive, I will never fly again.

Faster and faster, Bertha and I bump and rattle forward over the stubble field. Is it fast enough? Gently, I pull back on the stick. Bertha's nose rises. We hop about ten feet before Bertha comes back to earth with a shuddering thump. Not fast enough. I pull out the throttle. The engine note rises and Bertha surges forward, bumping wildly. I pull back on the stick again, praying that we are going fast enough this time. The fence at the end of the field is rushing toward us with terrifying speed. Then there are no more bumps. Bertha's wheels clear the fence by a good two feet.

"Woo-hooooooo!" I yell into the rushing wind. I'm flying!

When I look over the side at a couple of startled cows twenty feet below me, my knee knocks the stick to the right and Bertha wobbles alarmingly. I forget the cows and concentrate on keeping the machine stable and gently climbing—one hundred feet, two hundred, three hundred, four hundred. At about five hundred feet, I level off and risk a look around.

The world is spread out forever beneath a magical blue sky. The patchwork of fields, the grid of roads and tracks, the railroad with its scattered grain elevators disappearing toward the horizon, and the farmhouses nestled in their windbreaks of trees make me think of the imaginary landscape I used to create for my toy soldiers. But this is real. The roar of the engine, the whistling of the wind in the wire struts, the cold air tugging at my cheeks and making my eyes water—all are as real as the feel of Abby's saddle under me as I ride around the farm. I'm flying.

I laugh out loud and begin to play. I speed up and slow down. I climb and dive, turn, slide left and right, tilt my wings to look down at the ground beneath me. At first I wobble all over the place and almost stall a

couple of times—Bertha is very sensitive to any movement of the controls—but I force myself to remember
Horst's advice and picture the three axes running
through me. I imagine my body rotating around those
axes as I manipulate the controls—yaw, pitch and roll.
It's hard, but I gradually feel more comfortable. I do
everything gently, moving the controls tiny fractions
and correcting as soon as I feel apprehensive. Horst was
right—without him in the cockpit, Bertha is much
lighter, faster and more responsive. I resist the temptation to see how fast she can go or how high she can
climb. The last thing I want is to rip one of her wings
off or plummet to the ground in a stall.

I wonder if lads my age are flying like this over the
battlefields in Europe. Dad was right when he said the
fighting wouldn't be over by Christmas, and aeroplanes
have proved important—one spotted the German
army's swing away from Paris in September of last
year, making the miraculous victory in the Battle of
the Marne possible, and only yesterday the newspapers were full of Lieutenant Warneford's magnificent achievement in bringing down a Zeppelin by
dropping bombs on top of it. I pretend that I'm spotting the German army preparing for an attack, dropping bombs on grey-clad soldiers and shooting down
an enemy plane. What I don't do is remember one

important thing—I'm actually travelling over the ground at forty miles an hour.

When I eventually settle into level flight and look down, I recognize nothing. I strain to look back over my shoulder, but there is no sign of Horst's farm. I've no watch and have lost track of time. I could be many miles from home. I'm completely lost.

No need to panic, I think. All I have to do is turn around and head back the way I came. I took off to the north, so if I head south, I'll be fine. Very carefully, I execute a wide turn and fly in what I am sure is the right direction, scanning the ground for a familiar landmark.

As time passes, I become more and more nervous. It seems as if I've been flying for hours. All around me are fields, tracks and farmhouses, but none of them is the one I'm looking for. What if my maneuvers have gotten me completely turned around? What if I'm flying east or west, or even north? How much fuel does Bertha carry? Not much. How long have I been flying? Too long.

"Don't panic," I say out loud. "You can work this out. This is Saskatchewan. The roads and tracks between the fields run either north to south or east to west. If I align myself with them, then at least I'll be flying toward one of the cardinal points of the compass."

I look down. I'm flying diagonally across the square fields. Slowly I turn until I'm flying along a road. Now where's the sun? Above me and slightly ahead. That's good. It's early afternoon, so I'm heading south. But how far have I drifted? The breeze is pushing me from the west, and if I'm now flying south, that means I've been flying diagonally to the east. Horst's farm and the field where he is waiting could be far off to the west. Should I head more in that direction? Have I missed the farm already? How much fuel do I have left?

Then I see the grain elevators—two of them, rising like medieval fortresses from the flat prairie. Where there are grain elevators, there is a railway line, and I know the railway line runs just south of Horst's farm. As I approach, I recognize Mortlach, nestled as if for protection at the foot of the elevators. I give a cheer and turn Bertha along the main street. People look up, searching for the source of the noise. I wave, and some wave back. I head due west along the train tracks. Now I only have to worry about my fuel.

I see the red material flapping before I spot Horst's farm. My uncle is standing in the middle of the field, waving a horse blanket wildly above his head. I line up my approach and begin my descent. The engine coughs and a puff of black, oily smoke sweeps past me. I'm running out of fuel, but I can't worry about that. It takes all my concentration to slow my speed without stalling and keep Bertha level. I adjust the throttle and carefully wiggle the stick to keep the wings parallel to the ground.

The engine coughs again and I breathe in a lungful of foul smoke. There's the fence! I clear it by inches as the engine dies. The wheels hit the ground with an almighty thump, and something underneath me cracks loudly. Bertha bounces back into the air and I wrestle with the stick to regain control. The second time we don't bounce as high, and eventually, like a sick frog, we bump to a halt.

I sit for a moment, shaking and unable to force my hand off the control stick. Horst pounds across the field toward me. "What are you trying to do?" he asks breathlessly when he arrives. "Fly to Saskatoon?"

I look at him. It seems as if worry, anger and relief are fighting for control of his face.

"I'm sorry," I say. "I didn't pay attention."

"You must always pay attention," he says. His facial muscles decide to settle on a smile. "It is good, though. Ya?"

"It's breathtaking," I say, beaming back at him. "The most incredible, astounding, magical thing I have ever done."

"Ya, I know." Horst's smile is almost splitting his face. "It is all that and more. But come, we must put Bertha into the barn. There is a storm coming this evening. Then we will have some cold lemonade and sausage. And you can tell me of your adventure."

Stiffly, I climb out of Bertha's cockpit. I feel unsteady, as if out of my natural element. Gravity is pulling me down. The earth is holding me fast. My body feels like lead, trapped by its own weight. I feel bound to the ground below my feet. I stare at the blue sky, where dark thunderheads are already beginning to form on the western horizon. How will I manage until the next time I'm able to soar weightless with the birds? At that moment, I realize that I will never be truly content as long as my feet are anchored to the ground. True happiness can only be found in the air above my head.

CHAPTER 4

A Decision and a Gift—June 1915

"It was astonishing, thrilling, exquisite, enchanting!" I collapse into laughter, my supply of superlatives exhausted. "I felt like a god." We're sitting on Horst's porch, sipping tall glasses of ice-cold lemonade. The air is heavy and humid, and dark clouds are rolling up from the western horizon.

Horst grins broadly. "Ya. I felt exactly the same, the first time I went up alone."

We sip our drinks and watch the clouds grow.

"You are going to the war, now that you can fly?" Horst asks eventually.

"Yes," I reply. "As soon as I'm old enough, I will be a pilot."

"Canada does not have an air force," Horst points out.

"I know. But I will go to Britain and join the Royal Flying Corps. Dad is English."

"An expensive proposition."

"I'll manage," I say defensively, although I have no idea how.

"Hmm." Horst looks at me and strokes his chin. "Have you spoken with your father on this?"

"Not yet," I admit, "but I will."

"And do you know that the Royal Flying Corps will not accept anyone without a pilot's license?"

"Then I'll get one."

"That too costs money."

Suddenly angry, I slam my lemonade glass on the table between us and stand up. "If all you can do is point out the obstacles, then I'm going home."

"Sit down," Horst says gently before I've taken a step. His calm tone of voice and the half smile on his lips drain the anger from me as quickly as it appeared.

"I'm sorry," I say, propping myself against the porch rail. "That flight today was the most incredible thing I have ever done. Joining the Royal Flying Corps will allow me to follow my dream *and* do something for my country in the war."

Horst nods. "If I were your age, I would feel exactly the same. But it seems to me that you have four difficulties: a pilot's license, the money to get that license and travel to England, your age, and persuading your father to let you go."

"I know." I sit back down. The path to my dream seems impossible when the difficulties are laid out like that.

"Do not look so miserable," Horst says. "Difficulties are put in our way to be overcome. And some are easily dealt with. For example, did you know that the Royal Flying Corps accepts pilots at the age of seventeen?"

"I'll be seventeen in a few months."

Horst nods. "And with some other difficulties, I may be able to assist. I could talk to your father, for instance."

"That would be great," I say. "But why will you help me go to war?"

Horst looks at me for so long that I begin to feel uncomfortable. "There are two reasons," he says eventually. "First, you are young and strong-willed. You will find a way to follow your dream regardless of what your father and I say or do. Standing in your way will only make you angry at us."

I open my mouth to deny it, but before I say anything, I realize he's right. I *will* go somehow, regardless of how difficult it may be.

"Second," Horst continues, "already some people are saying we will have to bring in conscription."

"What's conscription?"

"A law that would force all men of a certain age to become soldiers. It will not happen this year, but the war will not end this year either. It will be better for you to join voluntarily. Then you will have the choice of doing what you want and are good at, rather than being just a soldier like all the others."

"And you will tell my father all of that?"

Horst nods once more. "I will. Also, I know of a small flying school outside Glasgow, just across the border in Montana. I know the owner, and we have communicated for many years on the subject of flying machines. I am sure he would take you."

"Which only leaves the money," I say, overwhelmed by the speed with which things appear to be moving. "Thank you."

"There is another reason I will help you, Edward," Horst says, staring into the distance. "Martha and I have not been blessed with children. You are the closest to a son that I have." My uncle blinks rapidly a number of times and I shift uncomfortably in my chair at Horst's unusual display of emotion. "I mean it when I say that you have a talent, Edward. I have never seen anyone take to flying the way you have. It is *your* dream, as it was mine. I cannot stop you going to war, but I can help feed your dream."

Thunder rumbles in the distance.

"The storm comes," Horst says gloomily. He turns to look at me. "If you wish, I will send a letter to my friend in Glasgow and talk with your father."

"Yes, please," I say softly.

Horst nods as if I am merely confirming what he already knows. "Then go and saddle your horse. I do not think it would be fitting if the world-famous flyer was struck by lightning on his way home."

I stand and look down at my uncle. There is a tear in the corner of his eye. "Thank you," I repeat.

"Ya, ya. Thank me when this is all over." He hauls himself out of his seat. "You wait here," he orders, disappearing into the house.

A moment later he returns carrying a small, rectangular black box.

"You are determined to go to war?" he asks.

"I am," I say.

"Well, then. I give you this for luck."

Carefully, I open the box. Nestled on deep red velvet is an ornate blue-and-gold cross. The top arm of the cross has a crown and the letter *F*. The other three arms have the words "Pour le Mérite" written on them in gold letters.

"It's beautiful," I say.

"Ya. My father won it in the war against France in 1870. It is the Pour le Mérite, Germany's highest military honor. Very rare."

"What did he win it for?" I ask, turning the wonderful object over in my hand.

"He captured an entire troop of French dragoons at the Battle of Sedan. In doing so, he was wounded—a

bullet through his right lung that left him always short of breath."

"I can't accept this," I say. "It's too valuable."

"What is the value of a piece of metal with some blue enamel on it? It is people who are important, and maybe this will bring you luck in whatever adventures you meet with."

"Thank you," I repeat.

Horst waves dismissively. "Thank me when the Pour le Mérite brings you back. Now go."

I close the box, tuck my new treasure into my pocket and walk to the barn. I saddle Abby and, with a final wave to the figure on the porch, head out onto the road. My emotions are in utter turmoil. Joy, excitement, sadness, confusion, fear—all fight for my attention. But there is one thing I am certain of: today is the most important day of my life. Everything I have been doing for my first sixteen years is finished. I don't know where the road in front of me is going, but I am certain it is a different path from the one I have been on. In a single day, I have realized my dream of flying and decided to go to war.

CHAPTER 5

Back to School—July 1915

"Okay, so how much flying you done?" Ted Barnham is a big, gangly redheaded guy. Oddly, on this hot July morning only two weeks after my conversation with Horst, he is wearing a heavily padded jacket, scarf, boots and a cloth cap set backward on his head. I feel underdressed in my patched sweater, canvas work pants and scuffed shoes.

"I've made five solo flights in Bertha," I reply. Ted and I are walking across a field at his aero school outside Glasgow, Montana, toward a large, sturdy biplane. The plane's fuselage is enveloped in doped fabric, and the engine is covered by a broad, smooth cowling. Solid wooden struts hold the wings together and support the two wheels. Strong wires run out to control the ailerons on the upper and lower wings, as well as the elevators and rudder on the tailfin. The engine cowling is painted silver, the wings a light tan and the fuselage a bright green. The plane is beautiful.

"Bertha'd be Horst's latest invention?" Ted asks.

"Yeah, his seventh, I think. She's a monoplane."

"Like a Blériot?"

"Yeah."

"Did you crash her?"

"No," I say indignantly.

Ted laughs. "Good, 'cause I don't want you wrecking my Avro 504."

"I won't," I say with more confidence than I feel.

"Good," Ted says again. "Fortunately, the 504's as stable as a battleship." We've reached the plane now, and Ted's pointing out features to me. "She's powered by a French Gnome rotary engine. The whole engine turns when it's running—all seven cylinders flying around. Scared the bejeezus out of me first time I saw it, but it gives you a lot of power, enough to do a full loop. Can you fly a figure of eight?"

"I've never done one, but I've done turns."

"Ever do a landing with the power off?"

"Once," I say, swallowing in embarrassment. "But that was because I wasn't paying attention and ran out of fuel."

Ted laughs. "I'll bet Horst doesn't bother with luxuries like a fuel gauge. Well, that's all you need to do for a license, so you're near enough there. Let's have a look in the cockpit."

We walk around and peer into the rear cockpit. I'm amazed at the complex of dials and levers.

"Bit fancier than Horst's?" Ted asks, seeing my jaw drop. "Rear cockpit's where the pilot sits, front's for the student. You recognize the rudder bar and the control stick?"

"Yes," I say, "but that's all."

"Horst's plane have a throttle?"

"Yes," I reply. "Why do you ask?"

"Well, a rotary engine don't need a throttle. Engine runs at full power all the time."

"How do you slow it down?"

"These here." Ted points to two small levers on the instrument panel. "The right one's called the blip switch, and it stops the fuel flow to the engine. You don't want to use that one much—it'll cause the spark plugs to clog, and she might not start again. Only use the blip switch when you're coming in to land. The other one's the air valve, and it adjusts the fuel-to-air ratio to the engine. The engine keeps spinning, but you reduce or increase the power. Simple."

I have my doubts, but I don't say anything.

"Those three dials"—Ted points above the switches —"will help you once you're aloft. Left one tells you your speed through the air. It's pretty accurate, as far as I can tell. Right one tells you the speed your engine's turning at. Not much use, since you're running a rotary flat out most of the time anyway. Middle one gives you your height above the ground, or it's supposed to. I never reckoned it worked too well. Better to look over the side and judge for yourself."

"What's that?" I ask, pointing to a ball that seems to float in some liquid behind a glass dial.

"That tells you if you're flying level. Useful if you can't see the horizon. The line across the middle's an artificial horizon, so the ball tells you how level you are. And you'll find these useful." Ted indicates two vertical glass tubes, almost full with a pale amber liquid. "They'll tell you if you're about to run out of fuel. There's two fuel tanks—a big one in behind the engine and a small gravity one on top of the wing." He points to a long silver tube above my head. "The level in the glass tube tells you how much is left in each tank, and the levers below allow to you switch off the fuel and move from one tank to the other."

"It's amazing," I say, taking in the dials, the polished wood controls and the leather seat.

"She's a beauty, right enough. But the front's not quite so fancy," he says, moving to the forward cockpit. "Same rudder and stick controls, but none of the impressive array of dials. Only the air valve and blip switch to control the engine. Probably looks more like what you're used to."

"It does," I say, looking in at the sparse cockpit interior.

"One more thing: these rotary engines take a lot of oil and spit it out once it's been used. That's why there's these windshields, but some oil always gets past. Two problems with that. One, the oil's hot, so you have to wear goggles at all times. Two, it's castor oil. You know what that does if you swallow it?"

"I do," I say, remembering too many times spent perched in the outhouse after my mother had given me castor oil for an upset stomach.

"Best to keep your mouth shut if the oil's coming at you," Ted advises. "Well, put these on and hop in." He hands me a pair of worn leather motorbike goggles. "Let's take her up for a spin."

He doesn't need to ask me twice. I begin to clamber into the front cockpit, but Ted stops me with a hand on my shoulder.

"You take the back one," he says. "Might as well get used to all the fancy stuff."

"You sure?" I ask, daunted by the prospect of having to watch all the dials.

"Sure," Ted says cheerily. "I've got controls up front to get us out of trouble if you mess up. And I think you'll find the 504 a bit more forgiving than Horst's contraptions. What height have you flown at?"

"Five hundred feet, tops," I reply.

"There's another thing," Ted says. "We'll head up to three thousand or so. A bit cold, but much safer up there. If anything goes wrong, there's time to fix it. And if you can't, you're just as dead from five hundred as you are from three thousand. Don't forget to strap yourself in!"

Ted fires up the engine and climbs in the front cockpit. With his instructions coming through the improvised speaking tube, I take off, nervous but thankful that I remembered to stuff Horst's Pour le Mérite into my pocket.

Ted's right—the Avro flies like a charm. The controls are much heavier than the ones in Bertha, but she feels solid and reliable. We climb steadily until the world looks very far away. I know I'm much safer up here, but it's scary nonetheless.

Following Ted's instructions, I twist and turn, climb and dive, and only occasionally feel his pressure on the stick, correcting me slightly. The windshield and my position in the rear cockpit stop most of the castor oil from reaching me, but an occasional spray of hot droplets stings my cheeks. I keep my mouth firmly shut. I'm freezing and my teeth are chattering, and I now envy Ted's heavy jacket. But despite the discomfort, I'm having a wonderful time. This is freedom.

"You're doing great," Ted's voice comes through the tube. He sounds very far away and has to shout against the noise of the engine and the wind. "Let's do a loop."

"What?" I yell back, thinking I must have misheard him.

"Let's loop-the-loop," Ted repeats.

"I can't," I say, terrified of the idea of being upside down.

"You'll have to do one sooner or later, and there's no time like the present. I'll take over if you get into difficulty. What does your altimeter say?"

"Three thousand five hundred," I say.

"Good enough. When I give the word, dive. Keep going till the speed builds up to one hundred, then pull back on the stick to climb. Not too fast or you'll stall us. It's a bit unnerving losing sight of the ground and the first time, you'll want to pull out of the loop too soon. Don't, 'cause you'll spin. Keep the stick pulled back until you can see the horizon again, then cut the engine way back with the airflow lever. Keep the stick a bit to the left. The rotary engine spins to the right, so it wants to pull you that way. Easy does it and you'll come round nice as anything. Don't panic, and remember, I've got controls here. I'll keep you right."

"All right," I say, although I feel far from all right. What am I getting myself into doing crazy stunts thousands of feet in the air with an insane American?

I fly along, trying to pluck up my courage.

"Whenever you're ready," Ted shouts.

I check that my harness is securely fastened, take a deep breath and push the stick forward. The needle on the airspeed dial jumps off the sedate fifty it's been sitting on and begins to climb.

Sixty—I push the stick forward more.

Seventy—What if the wings fold? I'll have a long time knowing I'm going to die before we hit the ground.

Eighty—Why don't I simply ease up, fly home and forget this madness? Because I'd be letting Ted and Horst down, and if I'm honest, beneath the fear there's excitement.

Eighty-five—The wind is violent and icy cold.

Ninety—The Avro's shuddering horribly. She's about to break apart.

Ninety-five—Ted has the other stick. He's got hold

of it. He's doing all this, and I'm simply following his movements.

One hundred—I pull back on the stick. The shuddering stops and the earth whips out of my view. There's nothing but sky around me. I've flown off the earth. I pull back on the stick more and climb and climb and climb. We must be over by now, but I still see nothing but sky. Maybe we've gone into a spin. Maybe I'll suddenly see the earth rushing up to meet us. What made me think flying was safe? And I haven't even got to the war yet! Don't be silly. Ted's got the stick. He's had it all along. He's in control, and I'm not in any danger.

As if by magic, the horizon appears in front of and above me. Keeping the stick back, I reach forward and reduce the airflow. The engine note drops, making the wind sound much louder. We come all the way round and level out at a sane speed.

"Woo-hooooooo," I scream into the wind. That was the most incredible thing I have ever done. "That was great," I shout into the tube. "Thank you, Ted!"

"Hey, don't thank me, kid. You did it, and real well too."

"What do you mean? You had the stick."

"Nope." Even distorted by the tube and the wind, the laughter in Ted's voice is unmistakable. "Never touched it. You did that all on your own."

"Really! I looped all on my own?"

"Sure did."

"Yippee!" I yell.

"Don't get too cocky," Ted says. "You've still got to get us down. And we'll never manage that if you don't remember to up the airflow again."

We fly around in a huge circle and come in to land. Following Ted's instructions, I flip the blip switch and we come into the field over the trees. It's a hard landing, and we very nearly crash on my third heavy bounce across the ground.

"Well, there's still work to be done," Ted says after we have parked the Avro, "especially on landings, but you did well. A couple of hours tomorrow and I don't see why I can't give you your license. Congratulations." He shakes my hand. "You're a natural. Them Germans better watch out when you get over there."

I head for the bunkhouse where my bedding is set up. I'm tired, both emotionally and physically. The raw excitement of looping the loop has gone, but I'm deliriously, stupidly happy. In only a few weeks, I've achieved a major part of my dream. I'm a pilot.

CHAPTER 6

Friends at Sea–September 1915

"What is that idiot doing?" Cecil asks in his high-class English accent. I'm standing with my new friends, Cecil and Alec, at the rail of the SS *Akrotiri* as we steam past the south coast of Ireland. These are dangerous waters; the RMS *Lusitania* was torpedoed and sunk not far from here back in May, so we're traveling as fast as we can. But the battered old freighter we're staring at is almost stationary in the water.

"Hun submarine'll get her for sure," Alec comments in his strong Newfoundland accent. Cecil and Alec are as different as chalk and cheese, but the three of us have become close friends on the journey from Canada.

After I returned home from Glasgow, proudly clutching my pilot's license, I faced the daunting task of persuading my parents to let me go to war. Horst had been working on Dad while I was away, so he was not a problem. Mom, on the other hand, was less keen on my adventure. "Next year, when you're eighteen, is early enough," she said.

I wasn't making much progress with her until Ted arrived to visit Horst. He roared in with the Avro one sultry afternoon and bounced to a halt in our back field. My uncle was already over, and the two of them set to work on Mom. Horst explained that being a pilot was by far the safest occupation in the war, and Ted explained the rudiments of flying and built me up as the best student he had ever seen. Then he took Mom up for a spin. She returned to earth breathless and almost as much in love with flying as I was, and that evening I was allowed to draft a letter to the War Office in London, offering my services. Plans were made for my transatlantic voyage and for my time in London, where I would lodge with a cousin of Dad's. I left from Moose Jaw station, amid cheers and tears, only ten days later.

I met Cecil, a skinny man more than six feet tall and several years older than me, on the station platform as I changed trains in Toronto. He was struggling with a huge steamer trunk and I gave him a hand. "Thanks, awfully, old chap," he said, sounding as if his cheeks were full of plums. He sat next to me on the long train journey to Halifax. At first, his accent made me think he was just an upper-class English snob, but I was wrong. Cecil was certainly upper class, he came from a very old, well-connected family, but as the third son, he had been sent out to Canada to make his own way in life. He had been everywhere, working with fur trappers way up north, helping surveyors in the Rocky Mountains and seal hunting in Newfoundland. He had not settled at anything, however, and somewhere along the way he'd learned to fly, so the war was a perfect opportunity for him to return to Europe and find some excitement. He's as determined to be a pilot as I am, and we spent many happy hours on the train talking about our shared love of flying, the unfettered joy we both felt being at three thousand feet and our plans to contribute to the war effort.

I met Alec on board the *Akrotiri*. He's Cecil's opposite, a rough and ready miner who's barely five foot four and powerfully built. He's on his way to join the Newfoundland Regiment in Egypt.

"That old rust bucket," Cecil says as we continue to stare at the freighter. "He cannot be doing more than a couple of knots. The poor chap's a sitting duck if there are any U-boats around."

As if in response, a sleek shape breaks the calm surface beside the laboring freighter. "My heavens!" Cecil exclaims. "Look at that chap. On the surface in broad daylight as bold as brass."

Soldiers and sailors are shouting all around us, and dozens of men are rushing to the rail to watch the unfolding drama. Our ship's whistle is sounding harshly. "Why'd he not just torpedo him?" Alec asks. "I thought that's what submarines did."

"Indeed they do," Cecil says as we watch hatches open on the U-boat's deck and tiny black figures rush to man the forward gun. "But this way he saves a torpedo. The freighter's not a threat and we're unarmed, so he can attack us at his leisure."

Suddenly what I am watching becomes less of an interesting show and more of a threat.

"Will he attack us?" I ask nervously.

"If he can dispose of that chap quickly enough," Cecil says. He seems remarkably calm amid all the shouting and running about. "Our best chance is to get far away while he's busy. I doubt if he's fast enough to catch us."

I look up at our three funnels, each one belching black smoke, and imagine the stokers in the bowels of the ship shoveling coal into the boilers for all they're worth.

"What's he doing now?" Alec's question draws me back to the drama in front of us. Instead of trying to run, the freighter has turned its side to the submarine. With a loud clang that we can hear quite clearly over the water, a massive panel on the freighter's side drops down to reveal a gun much larger than the one on the U-boat.

The U-boat fires first, but its shell explodes harmlessly in a column of water some distance away. The freighter replies, and a much larger fountain erupts very close to the U-boat's side. A ragged cheer bursts from the sailors watching around us.

"They're giving up!" Alec shouts excitedly as men scurry across the submarine's deck back toward the hatches.

Just then, a second shell explodes beside the submarine, throwing several men into the water. The rest are below now, and the hatches close. The submarine's bow dips beneath the waves. "She's getting away!" someone yells. A third shell catches the U-boat about two-thirds of the way along its length. The rear section, which is still sticking out of the water, buckles awkwardly and the submerged bow rises up again.

"That one's broken her back," Cecil says quietly.

Silence spreads through the men as we watch the U-boat die. They're the enemy and they attacked us without warning, but men like us are dying a horrible death over there. The freighter continues firing, and the two sections of the submarine soon slide beneath the waves. Debris bobs in a slowly expanding oil slick. There are men there as well, dark with the heavy oil, waving weakly. Soon the waving stops.

Soldiers and sailors drift away from the rail, talking in low voices. "She's a Q-ship," Cecil says. "A decoy. Chap I know at the War Office told me about them. A Q-ship is an old freighter that looks like a soft target but has powerful guns hidden behind screens. You saw what happens when a U-boat surfaces."

We're each alone with our thoughts as we head around the deck. None of us feels like going below, knowing what might be lurking under the water.

"Those poor men," I say, unable to shake the image of the helplessly waving arms in the water.

"There's our first taste of war," Cecil says. "Horrible way to die. Proves we made the right choice chasing our dreams in the sky with the birds, eh, Edward?"

I nod agreement and silently hope that Cecil and

I are sent to the same squadron. Our shared passion for flying makes me regard him as almost family.

"They brought it on themselves, Eddie Boy," Alec says. "And personally, I'm glad that Q-ship was there to do the job, or else it might have been us floating around in the ocean."

"A good point, my Newfoundland friend," Cecil says.

"War'll be over soon, anyway," Alec says cheerfully, trying to lighten the mood. "Soon as the Newfoundlanders get into it. Everyone knows Newfoundlanders are the best fighters in the world."

THE Q-SHIP LOOKS HARMLESS BUT IT HAS POWERFUL WEAPONS HIDDEN FROM VIEW.

"Among themselves," Cecil says with a smile, and Alec nods acknowledgment.

"There are a few boys from St. John's on board," I say to Alec. "Have you met them?"

"They're city slickers," he scoffs. "Real Newfoundlanders live in the outports, like me. Coachman's Cove, up west of Notre Dame Bay—that's the place I come from. God's country, for sure."

"Never heard of it," Cecil says.

"Well," Alec says, "that just goes to show how uneducated you are. There's a mine there, up the inlet at Terra Nova—or at least there used to be. Copper mine, it was. That's where I worked." Alec is happy to talk, and Cecil and I are glad to listen. It takes our minds off what we have just seen.

"My dad worked over on Tilt Cove," Alec goes on. "That was before a lump of copper ore crushed his leg. Terra Nova opened up just after my tenth birthday, so that's where I went to work. It was either that or going out on the boats, and I never much liked the smell of fish. Besides, being short's an advantage for a miner. Trouble was the mine closed down this year, so my choices were the army or the fishing boats." Alec throws his arms wide. "So here I am, Eddie Boy, on my way to exotic Egypt to show the Turks what's what at Gallipoli. Maybe after that, I'll come and help you flyboys in France."

We talk and joke, and the memory of the U-boat soon fades. Two days later we dock at Liverpool and, amid promises to keep in touch and vows of undying friendship, go our separate ways.

CHAPTER 7

Going to the Right School—September 1915

I'm standing at the tail end of a long, slow-moving queue in a corridor on the sixth floor of the War Office in Whitehall, London—and I'm seriously disappointed. I had assumed I'd be the only one here. My dad's cousin, the oddly named Morley Somerset, met me at Liverpool Street railway station and took me to his home on the Underground, or "the Tube," as Londoners call it. A letter from the War Office was waiting for me there, and it instructed me to appear in three days' time for an interview.

I spent the three days wandering around in a daze,

overawed by the size, noise and bustle of London. In half an hour walking along Oxford Street, I saw more people than live in the whole of Moose Jaw. I was surrounded by horse-drawn carriages, motor vehicles and omnibuses—all clanking, rattling and wheezing their way around the congested streets. The buildings were black with soot and towered over me, giving me the feeling of being trapped in a dark maze. I missed Saskatchewan's wide-open vistas and couldn't wait to get in a plane and soar above the clamorous, teeming throng.

Now I'm stuck at the back of the snail-like queue of other hopeful recruits. It's well after lunchtime, and my stomach is rumbling with hunger and nerves. Just then, a door a long way down the corridor opens and Cecil appears. I'm thrilled to see him again and step out of line to say hello.

"Well, Edward," he says, grasping my hand, a broad grin splitting his face. "Utterly splendid to see you again."

"Were you accepted in the Royal Flying Corps?" I ask excitedly.

Cecil looks slightly confused by my question. "Of course. The recruiter's a terribly nice chap. He was a master at my school before I moved out to the colonies. I must dash, though—lunch with Father and I'm late already. See you at Brooklands. I shall have a word in the right ear and see if we can be stationed in the same squadron. Cheerio for now."

"Goodbye," I say as Cecil leaves. I have no idea where Brooklands is, but I'm delighted that my friend also wants us to be in the same squadron.

After an eternity of nervous waiting, I'm ushered into a high-ceilinged office. As I enter, I reach in my pocket and squeeze the box containing the Pour le Mérite for luck. If it works while I'm flying, it might work here.

A short, balding, bespectacled man in an immaculately pressed uniform is sitting behind a large, shiny desk. "Name?" he asks without looking up.

"Edward Simpson, sir," I reply.

"What school did you go to?"

The question confuses me, but I answer as best I can. "Mortlach School, sir."

The man raises his head and peers at me through thick lenses. Thinking he needs more information, I keep going. "It's about twenty miles west of Moose Jaw. I used to ride in every day on Abby. She's my horse."

I fall silent under the stony stare. Eventually the man says, "Where in creation is Moose Jaw?"

"Saskatchewan, sir."

Still the stony stare.

"Canada." We hadn't thought it necessary to mention this fact in the letter.

"Canada?" He repeats it as if he has a bad taste in his mouth. "So you're a colonial."

"My father's English," I say defensively.

"And what exactly does your father do?"

"He farms a quarter section west of town. Wheat, mostly."

"He farms wheat." Again the bad taste in the mouth. "Look, young man, you have applied to join the Royal Flying Corps, a service of the British military. The types of recruits we are looking for come from good schools and families. Their fathers most decidedly do not farm wheat. Good day."

The man returns his gaze to the papers on his desk, but I continue to sit in stunned silence. I've been dismissed because I'm Canadian. I feel anger rising.

"That's not fair," I say.

The man looks up and blinks. "You are not the right sort for the Royal Flying Corps. I suggest you try the army. Their standards are lower."

"I don't want to join the army," I say, standing up. The man looks vaguely surprised. I don't suppose he's used to mere colonials talking back to him. "What does the Royal Flying Corps do?" I ask.

"We fly—" he begins, but before he can say anything more I cut him off.

"*I* can fly."

"What can you fly?"

"I learned on a monoplane built by my uncle." I decide it's best not to mention Horst's German name.

"Ah, a homemade plane. I don't think that quite qualifies you for what we are doing."

"And an Avro 504. I took my pilot's license on that." I flatten the certificate Ted gave me on the desk. I'm certain the man has never heard of the Aero School of Glasgow, Montana, but Ted did a good job of making the certificate look impressive.

"I never knew there was a flying school in Glasgow," the man says to my surprise. "It must be new." He looks up. "Why didn't you say you learned to fly in Scotland?"

I realize he has missed the Montana bit of the license and thinks I trained in Glasgow, Scotland. But I'm not about to correct him. "Sorry, sir," I say, sitting back down.

"How many hours solo?"

I count those on Bertha, add the hours on the Avro and round up. "About twenty in total, sir."

A flicker of interest crosses the man's face. "Did you do a figure eight?"

"Yes, sir."

"And a power-off landing?"

"Yes, sir."

"Hmm." The man scratches his neck thoughtfully and looks back down at my license.

"I can loop-the-loop, sir," I say, hoping to distract him before he notices that I've never set foot in Scotland. His head jerks up and his eyebrows raise in interest.

"In a 504?"

"Yes, sir."

The man closes his eyes and rubs his temples. I'm more nervous now than I was looping the Avro. This is my chance. If I haven't persuaded him, I've nothing left.

"Very well," the man sighs and opens his eyes. He scribbles something on a piece of notepaper. "Report to Captain George at Brooklands in three days' time." He hands me the paper. "And here's a chit for the rail fare."

"Thank you, sir." I stand and suppress the urge to salute. "I won't let you down, I promise."

"You'd better not," the man says. "On your way out, send in the next applicant. Perhaps *he* went to a decent school."

"Yes, sir."

I don't think my feet touch the ground as I walk down the corridor past the long line of hopeful applicants. I smile at everyone. I squeeze the Pour le Mérite in its black box. "Thank you," I murmur. I have difficulty not shouting out that I've been accepted. I'm going to be a pilot in the RFC. I'm going to war!

CHAPTER 8

The First Tragedy—January 1916

A fter a short spell at Brooklands, a motor-racing track near Manchester that has been taken over by the War Office and pressed into service as an aerodrome, I find myself at Gosport on England's south coast. Since arriving here, I've struggled to get used to the foul weather of England's southern coast, which keeps us sitting in damp tents for days at a time. Worse yet, our flying time is severely limited by the shortage of planes. But we have at least been lucky. It's said that more pilots die during training than are killed by the enemy over in France. We have had only four accidents and no deaths among our group.

The only joy outside of my scant time in the air is exploring the local countryside with Cecil. He knows a vast amount about the nature and history of England, and as we poke about in ancient churches, I learn much about the country my dad grew up in. I think that without Cecil by my side, I wouldn't be able to bear the loneliness and strangeness of my new life in this unfamiliar land.

Finally, I'm issued my smart new uniform and awarded the coveted wings of a fully trained RFC pilot to sew onto it. I spend Christmas in London with Morley, and in January we are shipped over the Channel to St. Omer in France for our final training. Cecil has been there for a couple of days before I arrive with five other new pilots one rainy, windswept morning. I'm looking forward to seeing him once more and finding out if he's managed to get us assigned to the same squadron. The first thing I do is ask for my friend, but I'm told he's up on a solo flight.

We six new arrivals line up outside a large hangar beside a collection of biplanes. In the distance, there is an odd-looking monoplane, its wing raised high above the fuselage so the pilot sits under it. What intrigues me is what appears to be a machine gun sitting on top of the engine. My attention is drawn away, however, as the base's commanding officer begins to address us.

"Welcome to France, gentlemen," he begins. He's a short man with a friendly face. He's not as neatly dressed as the officers I have become used to, and he walks with a limp. "St. Omer will be your home until you are transferred to an operational unit. You will each be assigned a B.E.2c." He waves his arm at the biplanes parked outside the hangar. "I suggest you take your plane up for practice at every available opportunity."

We are standing in a line and I am at the extreme right. The officer begins at the left.

"How many hours solo?" he asks.

"Fourteen, sir," the first pilot answers.

The officer shakes his head. "It's criminal sending pilots out with so little experience. Still, at least you survived the training."

He continues down the line. No one else has more than twenty hours of flying time. Finally, he stands in front of me.

"How many hours?"

"About thirty-six, sir," I answer.

He cocks his head and regards me with interest. "Where did you get all those?"

"I learned on my uncle's plane in Saskatchewan and then got my license on an Avro 504 at the Aero School in Montana. The last twelve were at Brooklands."

"So you've flown a 504. You'll have no trouble with the B.E., then. What was your uncle's machine?"

"He made it himself, sir," I answer.

One of the other pilots—an arrogant kid fresh out of one of the "right" schools in England—snickers.

The officer turns on him. "Arrogance will get you killed out here quicker than anything else," he warns. Then, turning back to me, he says, "Describe it."

"It looked a bit like that, sir." I point at the monoplane. "The wings came out of the fuselage, but high up. It had a fifty-horsepower inline engine and ailerons."

"How did it handle?"

"It was very light, sir. Much more sensitive than the Avro."

The officer stares at me for so long that I begin to feel very uncomfortable. "What's your name?" he asks eventually.

"Simpson, sir. Edward Simpson."

The officer nods and steps back. "All right," he says, addressing us all. "Go over and select a B.E. each, and then go to the quartermaster and draw equipment. Weather's not the best this morning, but we'll see what you can do this afternoon. Dismiss."

I begin to follow the others, wondering vaguely why Cecil's up flying in bad weather, when the officer calls me back. "Simpson, a word if you please." He limps

over to the monoplane and I follow, convinced I've done something wrong already.

"You know what this is?" he asks, indicating the plane. I shake my head. "It's called a Morane-Saulnier L. Everyone calls it the Parasol, on account of the high wing. French machine. Absolute devil to fly. One wrong move and you spin. Death trap for inexperienced pilots. We've two here. Other one's up at the moment."

READY FOR FLIGHT.

That must be the plane Cecil's flying, I think to myself. I peer into the cockpit. It looks normal enough, but the stick is very short and ends in a leather handgrip.

"Most planes'll fly level if you let go of the stick," the officer says. "Not the Parasol. You let go of that leather grip, the stick'll shoot forward and you'll go into the steepest dive you've ever seen. You need to be flying every second you're up there, and don't try anything, even a simple turn, at under five hundred feet. It's a rotary engine in a small plane. You have to fight to get the plane to turn against the rotation of the engine, but if you touch the stick the same direction as the engine rotation, she'll whip round before you know it. Useful in a dogfight. But overdo the controls and you'll be buried in a field before you know what happened. In the right hands, she's nimble." He steps forward and pats the cowling behind the propeller. "The engine's a reliable Le Rhône eighty-horsepower, so she's fast enough. A match for anything the other side has at the moment. In the right hands," he repeats, lifting his head to hold me with his gaze. "This one's yours if you want it."

I'm flattered at the offer, but terrified at what he's told me about the Parasol's dangers. I look back over at the comfortable biplanes and the other pilots milling around them.

"They're safer, no doubt," the officer says, seeming to read my mind. "But do you know what they call them at the front lines?"

I shake my head.

"You've heard of the Fokker Eindecker?"

"The German monoplane with the gun that fires through the propeller?"

"That's the one. It's fitted with an interrupter gear that stops you shooting the propeller off. We haven't come up with an answer to that yet, so anything that can't outmaneuver the Fokkers is in serious trouble. The old B.E.2c is fondly known as 'Fokker Fodder.'" The officer looks across at the other new pilots, laughing and messing around among the biplanes. A sad expression crosses his face. "Most pilots coming out here have no idea what to expect. They don't have enough training or good enough machines to compete with the German pilots. A frightening number of them are dead within three weeks." He looks back at me. "But if a pilot puts the hours in, the Parasol's a match for the Eindecker."

I'm shocked by what he's telling me. In an instant, the safe life I had imagined—flying free thousands of feet above the fighting—has vanished. Three weeks! But then I realize that maybe I'm being offered something more than a plane that sounds like a certain disaster. Maybe I'm being offered a chance to live.

"Does the Parasol have an interrupter gear, sir?" I ask, looking at the machine gun mounted in front of the cockpit. I recognize it as a Lewis gun by the round magazine on top.

The officer laughs. "Of a sort. Look." He points to a V of metal bolted to near the base of each propeller blade. "Those are deflector plates. With a two-bladed propeller like this, about one in ten bullets will hit a blade. The Vs are designed to deflect those bullets left or right. Puts a strain on the engine, but it works—most of the time. So do you want to try her out this afternoon?"

"Yes, sir," I say, hoping I sound more confident than I feel.

"Good. Now off you go and get kitted out."

"Yes, sir."

"Simpson, just one more thing."

"Yes, sir?"

"Less of the 'sir.' The RFC's less formal than the army—at least down here at the sharp end, where you're heading. For the most part, we don't go for the standing at attention, the saluting and the sir-ring. In private, we're all pilots." He holds out his hand. "My name's Jack."

I shake his hand and swallow the "yes, sir" before it slips out. "Thank you."

I'm turning away when I hear the sound of a plane approaching. It's the Parasol that Cecil's taken up. I'm excited that we'll both be the Parasol pilots. They'll have to send us to the same squadron now.

The officer and I are both scanning the sky. "There he is," Jack finally says, pointing. I follow his arm and see the tiny shape of the Parasol heading toward us. It's being thrown around by the wind and must be a bumpy ride for Cecil. "He's coming in too high and too far to the left," Jack mutters.

The Parasol's about a hundred feet above the trees and on a line off to one side of the runway.

"Remember the rotary engine," Jack says under his breath. "Don't try to bank right at that height. Go around and come in again."

The instant Jack stops talking, the Parasol's right wing dips sickeningly. With horrifying speed, the plane twists in the air, spins over and plummets straight down behind the trees. The noise of wood shattering reaches us over the wind.

All over the field, men have been watching the Parasol come in. Now several of them, including Jack, take off at a run toward the trees. I stay where I am, rooted to the spot by a sick feeling in my gut and the horrifying realization that my friend Cecil is dead.

ONE OF OUR PLANES AFTER A CRASH LANDING.

CHAPTER 9

A Pair of Letters—February 1916

ecil died instantly, his body crushed in the mangled remains of the Parasol. I spend the rest of the morning walking around the field in the rain, mourning the only friend I had in a thousand miles. I promise myself that I will not get close to anyone else in this war. That way I won't have to suffer the pain of loss again.

In early afternoon, the wind drops and the clouds break up. Jack insists that despite the tragedy of the morning, I take the remaining Parasol up. I remember nothing of the flight except a determination to make myself the best Parasol pilot in the war, as an honor to Cecil.

Over the succeeding days, I ignore the other young pilots struggling to master their cumbersome B.E.2cs. I get a reputation as a loner, but I don't care. I work hard with the Parasol and, with Jack's help and encouragement, learn to love it. Jack's right—the Parasol's fast and maneuverable, but you can't relax for a minute when flying it. Any of the dozens of mistakes I make in training would be fatal close to the ground, but at five thousand feet there is time to correct. I learn that the trick is not to try never to make mistakes, but to know how to correct them quickly when they happen.

"All right, you've got most of the basics," Jack says one morning. "Now you're ready to spin."

"If I spin, I'll crash," I say. "It was a spin that killed Cecil."

"Yes, a spin at two hundred feet above the ground. But if you've got enough time and space, there are ways to recover. Do you know what a spin is?"

"It's when the plane goes out of control and spirals down."

"But it happens because you stall. If your plane stalls, it will flip over on whichever wing has the most drag, making you spin left or right. Your instinct is to increase power and pull back on the stick to force your way out of the spin. But that's actually the worst thing you can do. When you go into a spin, make sure your ailerons are neutral, reduce power and give the machine hard rudder in the opposite direction—if you're spinning to the left, give hard right rudder and vice versa. As soon as you come out of the spin, ease off on the rudder and increase power. *Voilà*, you have control back. Want to give it a try?"

I nod, not trusting myself to speak. In next to no time, I'm following Jack up to five thousand feet. We've received a replacement Parasol for Cecil's machine and Jack takes that up. It's agreed that he will spin first and I will watch. As I circle, Jack climbs and reduces power. For an instant, his Parasol stands stationary on its tail. Then it tilts to the left and snaps into a terrifyingly tight spiral down. I follow and see Jack set the ailerons to neutral and move the rudder hard over to the right. The spiral eases and the Parasol is suddenly flying flat. Jack points up to indicate my turn and smiles. I take a deep breath to calm myself and pull the stick back.

I feel the Parasol losing power in the climb. Everything seems to be slowing down. I stop, hanging impossibly in the air, then, with a sickening lurch that leaves my stomach behind, my plane falls. The force of the spin presses me back into my seat, and the sky and the land flip wildly across my vision. I resist the temptation to pull back on the stick and try to think calmly. Following Jack's instructions, I neutralize the ailerons, reduce the power and kick the rudder hard over. Almost magically, I am flying level and under control. I look around and give him an enthusiastic thumbs-up.

Back on the ground, Jack congratulates me. "Now you don't need to be afraid of a spin. Most pilots are terrified of spinning. They think it's a death sentence. But it can actually save your life."

"How?"

"Imagine you're in a fight and you're losing. Say your Lewis gun's jammed and there's a Fokker on your tail." He shrugs. "Throw the Parasol into a spin. Chances are good the Fokker pilot will assume he's got you and go after someone else. Spin as long as you can, then level out and head for home."

I take Jack's lessons to heart and practice spinning until I'm confident going into one and coming out. I also learn to shoot well—all those hours hitting gophers on the farm have given me a good eye. Of course, a gopher sits still while you aim, unlike an enemy plane that's moving rapidly and unpredictably through three dimensions, but Jack assures me that a good eye is critical for a successful pilot. By the end of my training, I'm winning almost all my mock dogfights against the other pilots at St. Omer. I even manage to beat Jack once or twice.

At St. Omer I receive almost weekly letters from Mom giving me all the news from home, the gossip about our neighbors and the goings-on in Moose Jaw.

Sometimes the letters are in parcels containing knitted socks and tins of candy, and a couple of times Mom even persuades Dad to add a few curt lines at the end. I also receive two letters that I didn't expect. I'm delighted to receive them both, but the first contains bad news.

Hello Edward,

I hope that you are learning to fly well, and that Father's Pour le Mérite is bringing you luck. I envy you your youth and the chances you have to fly.

Poor Bertha is no more. I flew last month in too much cold and wind, and she landed in a tree instead of a field. But I am building another in the barn. I have many ideas on how I can run the wires to better control the flight. In the spring, Bertha will soar once more.

I am afraid now that I must pass on some sad news. Ted died some weeks ago. He was flying back from Bismarck and became caught in a storm. The wings came off the Avro and he fell in a field only a few miles short of his home. It is a great loss.

If you have time, please write and tell of the planes you have seen.

I wish you all the best,
Uncle Horst

I'm terribly sad to hear of Ted's death. He was very kind to me and taught me a lot. His accident brings home how dangerous flying is, even if you don't go to war.

Of course I write back to Horst immediately, telling him of my adventures, describing the machines I've flown and wishing him luck with the new Bertha.

The other letter is even more of a surprise and it's taken quite a while to find me. It's addressed simply to "Edward Simpson. Pilot. Royal Flying Corps. England."

Hello Eddie Boy,

I hope this reaches you and all is well.

I never got to Gallipoli. By the time I reached Egypt, the invasion force was being withdrawn, so I had to sit in Cairo and wait for them to return. The training here was boring, and I don't imagine it will be of much use in France, where we are headed next. I've put in a request for a transfer to the Royal Flying Corps, so maybe we'll meet up somewhere.

Cairo is a strange place. Everything and anything is for sale in the bazaars and the place is full of Australians, so it seems as if there's a fight every night. I saw the pyramids, though. They sure beat anything I ever saw in Coachman's Cove!

We board ships for Europe in a day or two, and I

don't know where I'll be after we arrive. Still, if this reaches you, try writing back c/o the Newfoundland Regiment. It should get to me eventually. I would like to hear your news.

Don't fall out of the cockpit!

I look forward to catching up and sharing a tale or two.

All the best,
Your friend, Alec

I'm glad Alec didn't make it to Gallipoli. I've heard stories about what a disaster it was over there. I write back giving my news and tell him I also hope we can meet up somewhere.

It's very strange getting letters from home and from Alec. They seem to be from a different world, and my world is about to change even more. Tomorrow, February 29 of this leap year, I am to travel south to Bapaume, to join No. 8 Squadron and the real war.

CHAPTER 10

The Canadian Kid—February 1916

Every bone in my body aches from hours spent in the back of a lorry bouncing over rough roads, but we have at last arrived. I am the only pilot joining this squadron. I climb down, retrieve my gear, wave goodbye to the driver and look around. I'm not sure what I expected, but this is certainly not it. London was indeed a shock for a farm boy from Saskatchewan, but everywhere I have gone from there seems to take me to an even stranger place. It has been a long journey, but now I'm almost at the war—and oddly, it looks more like home.

About a dozen single-seater Parasols are scattered haphazardly around a farmyard. The stone farmhouse looks abandoned, but there is activity around the large barn, with several figures coming and going. Tents of various sizes are spread around, and a few mechanics are working on a Parasol outside a ramshackle wooden hut. I assume that the closest field is the airstrip, but the only real clue is the worn grass in the center. My impression of having returned to Horst's back field is reinforced by the sight of a solitary cow placidly grazing nearby. A regimented line of plane trees runs along the country road and marks the end of the airstrip. Wondering what I'm getting into, I hoist my pack to my shoulder and head toward the barn.

I've got only about halfway when a terrifying racket breaks out. It sounds like an animal is being tortured, but the noise quickly resolves itself into a tune of sorts. A figure emerges from the barn and strides toward the airstrip, where it marches back and forth in the fading evening light. It's someone playing the bagpipes.

Feeling confused, I continue on. When I'm almost at the barn, a man detaches himself from a small group to my right and approaches. He's tall and skinny, and sports a thick mustache. Instead of a regulation uniform, he's wearing riding breeches and a tweed jacket with a bright green silk scarf knotted round his neck. He holds out his hand and smiles broadly.

"You must be the new chap."

I shake his hand. "Edward Simpson, sir."

"Oh, we don't much bother with the 'sir' thing here," he says with a dismissive wave. "Only if some of the top brass are coming—and they don't get out here much. I'm the CO, Captain Neville Fowler, but most of the chaps call me Wally. They think my facial hair makes me look like a walrus."

A particularly loud bagpipe tune interrupts him. I look over.

"Don't worry about Jock," Wally says. "He loves those bagpipes of his. Plays them every evening, whatever the weather. Even takes them up in the cockpit with him. Says they bring him luck on patrol. Some of us think they're his secret weapon. If his Lewis gun jams, he just plays the pipes and Fritz thinks a host of demons are after him."

"Who's Fritz?" I ask.

"That's just our nickname for the enemy—same as Jock's our nickname for our mad Scottish piper. But old Jock's not the craziest we have here. Come on in. Let me show you where your bunk is."

I've only just entered the barn when I'm startled by a loud thunk beside my head. I look round to see a long, evil-looking knife protruding from the wooden wall. On a very tattered sofa in the middle of the barn sits a massive bear of a man. He's dressed in uniform pants and a leather jacket, and has one leg thrown casually over the sofa's arm. He's cleaning his fingernails with the point of another knife.

"Meet Bowie," Wally says casually. "He's our American. Best we can do until his government sees the error of its ways and pitches in to help. He's good with a knife. In fact, some of the fellows think he would do better throwing knives at the enemy from his Parasol. That right, Bowie?"

"Might be," Bowie answers. Before I have a chance to collect my thoughts and say something, his arm snaps back and the second knife flies past my head and embeds itself in the barn wall beside its companion. "Don't worry, kid," Bowie says when I flinch. "I ain't hit anyone . . . yet."

I drop my pack and work the two blades out of the wood. As I hand them back to him, I say, "Whereabouts in the States are you from?"

"Kansas," he says in an exaggerated drawl as he takes the knives from me.

"So what are you doing over here in the RFC?"

"Was bored looking down on that flat prairie all the time. Thought I'd come and see what a bit of history looks like from up there." He jerks his thumb toward the barn roof. "But you're no limey yourself, kid."

"Canadian," I say.

"The Canadian Kid. This place's real international. Ever heard of a place called Moose Jaw?"

I can hardly believe my ears. "My dad's farm is thirty-five miles west of there."

Bowie hauls his leg back over the arm of the sofa and leans forward with interest. "Then you must know Horst."

"He's my uncle!" I say, amazed to hear his name here. "How do you know him?"

"Well, I'll be." Bowie jumps to his feet, and in two strides, he has me in a bear hug. When he lets me go, he looks me up and down. "This Canadian Kid is Horst's nephew," he says in wonderment, ignoring my question. "How is the old German?"

"He was fine, according to the last letter I received. How do you know him?" I repeat.

"Oh, he sent me a letter, must be seven or eight years ago now. He'd got my name from somewhere and knew that I had worked with the Wrights. He wanted to know how to build a flying machine." Bowie laughs, a deep, resonant sound. "Like it was some kid's toy. Still, I put him onto some things, and before I know it, he writes back to say he's flown his homemade machine. Strange name—Bessy or Bella, or something like that."

"Bertha," I say.

"Yeah, that's it. Bertha! Anyway, we've been writing back and forth ever since. I don't build my own machines, but Horst sure gave me lots of advice when it came to modifying the ones I had. Did he teach you to fly?"

"He did. Him and Ted down in Montana."

"Ted still run that flying school?"

"He did."

"Did?"

"He died a few weeks back. Went down in a storm coming home from Bismarck."

"Aw, now that's a shame. He was a good guy, and a fine pilot." Turning to Wally, Bowie says, "You look after the Canadian Kid. If he's half the flyer Horst is, he'll run rings around any of that crowd of lunatics you call a squadron." Bowie suddenly tilts his head to one side and listens. "Speaking of lunatics, here's one coming now."

I can't hear anything, but I follow the other two outside. The bagpipes have stopped and everyone is staring off to the east. Eventually I see a black dot against the darkening sky. The dot grows until I recognize it as a Parasol flying just above the treetops. Silence descends as the engine cuts and the Parasol glides in and bumps to a halt. Everyone rushes forward, but they stop when the pilot lifts his goggles onto his forehead, sticks his arm out of the cockpit and gives a thumbs-down. Grumbling, the others turn and head back to the barn.

"That's Mick," Bowie says as the pilot hauls himself out of his cockpit. "A mad Irishman, but a fine flyer. Right now he's the squadron's best chance of getting an ace. Only man here who actually enjoys the war. That right, Mick?"

"I'm thinking I should be back in Ireland fighting the English," Mick says. He's short and powerfully built, with a shock of ginger hair. "Now *that* I would enjoy. I got nothing against Fritz personally, but I didn't like the way he invaded Belgium without so much as a by-your-leave. We small countries got to stick together, and the Irish know what it's like to be invaded. And once you decide to fight, there's no point in going at it halfway. You don't start a fight, but if one breaks out, you fight to win."

Mick has carried on walking as he speaks and I can barely hear what he is saying by the end.

"See what I mean?" Bowie says. "Mad as a hatter. Thinks the kaiser was trying to annoy him personally by invading Belgium."

"What did you mean when you said Mick was the squadron's best chance of getting an ace?"

"An ace is someone who's shot down five enemy planes," Bowie explains. "Squadron's been here five months now. Be nice if we had an ace on the roster. I've got two kills; Wally and Jock, the bagpipe player, have three each. But Mick's got four. One more and he'll be an ace. We all want to get there, for the pride of the squadron"—Bowie winks at me—"and because you get leave when you reach five. Anyway, Mick's our best chance." His brow furrows in worry. "Trouble is, he's taking it too serious. He's always taken risks, but he's becoming obsessed. Goes up every chance he gets, flying deep over the lines looking for something. Does crazy things. Dangerous things. I've seen him come back with a lot less plane than he left with. We all pray that he gets number five soon." He looks uneasily at Mick's plane. "But listen to me, whining on about our problems when you just got here. Come on over to the barn and meet the others. And I want to hear some stories about Horst."

I follow Bowie back across the field, feeling overwhelmed. The talk of kills is jarring. I've thought a lot about shooting down enemy planes, but calling victories "kills" reminds me that there's another human being flying the opposing aircraft, even if he is a Fritz. I suppose it's something I'm going to have to get used to.

I also wonder if everyone in the RFC is as eccentric as the characters I've met here so far—a fanatical Irishman, a knife-throwing American and a Scot who takes his bagpipes on patrol for luck. Well, maybe the last isn't *that* crazy. After all, I plan to take Horst's Pour le Mérite up with me. I shrug. It doesn't matter. I'm here for better or worse. These are the men I'm going to have to live and fight with. This is my family from now on.

CHAPTER 11

The Immelmann Turn—March 1916

"Okay, Kid," Bowie says. In the past two weeks, my nickname has shortened from the Canadian Kid to simply Kid. We're standing in the dawn light beside two Parasols with their engines warming up. A fitter and a rigger—the mechanics whose job it is to keep the Parasols repaired and flying—stand beside each machine. "Keep your distance," Bowie instructs. "A couple of hundred yards behind and the same above. Never stop scanning the sky around you. I'll not be flying flat out, so if you see something, pull up beside me and point."

I've heard all this before, but this will be my first time flying over the trenches into enemy territory, so I listen hard. Most of the other pilots are out on reconnaissance duty. Bowie's idea is for us to go hunting, as Mick does on his own.

"You've done good so far," Bowie continues, "but this ain't the same as pretending to shoot me down. I plan to climb as high as these things'll go and see if we can surprise Fritz. Do exactly as I do, and if we get in a fight, try not to shoot me down. Get within one hundred yards of Fritz before you open fire, else you won't hit a thing." He turns to me and places a fatherly hand on my shoulder. "In a fight, you're not going to remember any of this. It all happens too quickly. Just don't let anyone get on your tail. Don't fly straight. Keep turning and keep looking. You ready, Kid?"

I nod and we climb into our machines. I've taken to tying Horst's Pour le Mérite to one of the exposed struts inside the cockpit. I figure that if it brings me luck in my pocket, it'll bring even more luck out in the open. We're all superstitious—Bowie takes his knives with him, Jock his bagpipes. Even Mick has a routine of walking round his plane three times and touching certain pieces before he climbs in. We all profess to believe it does no good, but we all do it every flight. Who knows?

I take off and climb into the lightening sky. At first I'm so nervous that all I can do is concentrate on keeping my position behind and above Bowie, but then I relax and look around. I've seen the front lines before— the zigzag network of trenches, the shell craters, the huge tethered observation balloons. It all looks so peaceful from up here. It's hard to believe that just below, tens of thousands of men are cowering in holes in the ground, unable to lift their heads without being killed. I smile as I watch the lines drift past below me. I am over enemy territory now. Odd how it looks the same. I abruptly remember where I am and start scanning the sky around me. There's little danger on our side of the lines—the Fokkers are forbidden to cross into our territory in case they crash and the secrets of their synchronized machine guns fall into our hands— but here . . .

My neck soon hurts from craning around. I don't need to look so often. Much as they're feared, the Fokkers aren't magical. They can't appear from nowhere. They have to approach us at about the same speed we're flying, so there's usually plenty of time to see them. I settle into the rhythm that Bowie has taught me, checking each quadrant of the sky systematically every thirty seconds or so. Often enough to prevent anyone from sneaking up on me.

Bowie waves his arm above the wing and indicates that he is going to turn. Gently we ease to the right until we are flying south, parallel to the line of observation balloons in the distance. The sun is rising in the sky to my left, a huge orange ball of fire that is painful to look at. I keep scanning. Then I see it—a biplane far below us and to my right, flying in a steady course parallel to ours.

I adjust the fuel mixture to speed up, then drop down until I am flying beside Bowie. I point to the biplane. I'm close enough to see Bowie smile. He points to his chest and holds up two fingers. It's one of ours, he's telling me—a B.E.2c. I feel like a fool. To gain altitude, I maintain my speed and begin a climbing turn away from Bowie. The sun is right in front of me, and something catches the edge of my vision. I complete my turn and scan. Nothing. Wait, there is something! A black dot at the bottom of the sun. I squint against the glare. The dot becomes a shape as it moves away from the sun. It's a plane, a monoplane, and it's diving toward the B.E. It's a Fokker, a hunter just like us!

I look for Bowie. He's below me and behind. After my turn I forgot to reduce speed and I've overtaken him. By the time I slow and drop into formation beside him, it'll be too late for the B.E. I make a snap decision and drop the Parasol's nose into a dive toward the Fokker.

Bowie quickly picks up what I'm doing. Before I get to the Fokker, he flashes over me with a wave. I try to keep up and watch. The German pilot is focused on his prey and hasn't seen us. Bowie's on the German's tail and closing fast. Why doesn't he fire? He wants to get close enough to be certain. I'm almost holding my breath. Finally, I hear the rattle of his Lewis gun. At the same instant, the German pilot flips the Fokker into a twisting, diving loop. In a flash, he's reversed direction and is flying straight at me. He isn't expecting me to be here, and I'm close enough to see the shocked look on his face. I fire my own Lewis gun. The Fokker roars past only feet above me. Something splashes onto my windshield. Oil! I must have hit him. I strain to look back and see the Fokker spinning out of control. I watch until it hits the ground in a tiny puff of dust. I try not to think that there was a man in that plane.

Bowie is beside me, grinning and waving a thumbs-up. He points toward home. I turn to follow him, still stunned by what has happened. I've shot down an enemy plane on my first sortie across the lines! The thrill is almost as great as going solo the first time or looping the loop. I whoop with delight, and then remember that we're not home yet and return to scanning the sky.

Bowie lands first, and by the time I stop my plane outside the barn, a crowd has gathered. Everyone wants to shake my hand and pat me on the back. Only Mick holds back, staring sullenly from the shadows of the barn door.

"Well done, Kid," Bowie says, clasping me in his trademark bear hug. "And you got the mark of an ace on your windshield."

I look at the dark spots as Bowie releases me. "I must have hit him in the engine to get splashed with oil like that."

"Oil?" Bowie laughs. "That's not oil, Kid. That's blood. The mark of an ace is to get close enough to get blood on your windshield from the kill."

A wave of nausea overwhelms me, and I fall to my knees and retch on the ground. I feel Bowie's arm round my shoulder.

"It's always bad the first time, Kid. You'll get used to it."

Will I?

"That, Kid, was an Immelmann turn." Bowie and I are sitting on an overstuffed sofa in the middle of the barn. High wooden partitions mark off bunk space for the pilots around the walls, but the center is a communal area. It's furnished with a wild assortment of articles:

the sofa, various chairs, a long oak table and several standard lamps with wires trailing across the floor to a generator outside. At one end, several pilots are congregated round a scuffed pool table. The others lounge about, reading or talking. The wall behind the pool table is decorated with broken propellers, fragments of planes and pieces of fabric bearing numbers or, in one case, a black Maltese cross. This is our trophy wall, a place to display whatever mementos pilots have been able to salvage from their victories.

"What's an Immelmann turn?" I ask. I'm still feeling confused by this morning's events, but Bowie and the others have assured me that it's a common reaction, and that I'll soon get over it. The feeling of being part of a close-knit group is powerful. Only Mick hasn't shaken my hand.

"It's named after Max Immelmann, the German ace. He invented it as a way of turning on your opponents to get a second attack in, but as you saw, it works when you're in trouble too. Or it would have if you hadn't been following along behind me." Bowie thoughtfully scratches the stubble on his chin. "How do you feel about becoming a team?"

"A team?"

"Yeah. You and me. Like this morning. You're a good flyer, Kid. You've got a natural instinct. With a bit of practice and a long enough life, you could become a great ace." He looks over at Mick, who's on his bunk staring at the ceiling. "We've always hunted alone—especially him. But things're changing. Fritz is beginning to hunt in packs. If you're on your own and you come up against Immelmann and a couple of his buddies, you won't stand a snowball's chance in hell of getting home. But if there's two or three or four of us, we could make a fight of it."

"Sounds like a good idea," I say.

"Okay, then. I'll run the idea by Wally and see what he says."

A loud wail sounds from outside. Groans echo round the barn.

"I swear," Bowie says, "if Fritz doesn't get that Scotsman, I'll shoot him myself before this war is over."

CHAPTER 12

An Ace at Last—April 1916

For two weeks it rains steadily. It's all we can do to keep dry and stop our planes from rotting. There's very little flying. Then, on April 1, we wake up to clear skies.

"Come on, you lazy lot," Wally shouts, rattling a stick along the wall of the barn. We crawl out of our bunks as the generator coughs to life and our lights flicker on. "It's a perfect day for flying, and we want to get in the air by sunrise. HQ want some photographs of our section of the Hun's trenches to see what he's been up to in the past two weeks. Usual pattern. Three parallel lines along the front—A above their trenches, B back over the reserves and C over their artillery. We're to provide cover for three B.E.2cs. We rendezvous with them in an hour."

It's a tense moment because no one wants line C. With lines A and B, you have at least a fighting chance of getting back over our territory if you're forced down. With line C, if you survive the fight, you're a prisoner.

"Now, we're going to do this a bit differently today," Wally explains as we each struggle into our flying kit. "Bowie has this idea that we should fight in groups, and I think it's a good one. We don't have a lot of planes, but there will be two over each of the 2cs."

Wally and an Englishman he knows from school take line C, the most dangerous one. Despite his protests that he fights alone, Mick is assigned to the B line with Jock, and Bowie and I are given A. I suspect I'm put on the safest line because I'm the newest recruit.

"You will fly as high as possible above the 2cs you are protecting. Keep your eyes peeled and stay in formation. Your responsibility is to the plane below you." Wally looks pointedly at Mick. "You will not go off searching for glory and leaving your charge unprotected. What's important are the photographs and getting them back safely. This is the first clear day in a while. It doesn't take a genius to work out that we'll be

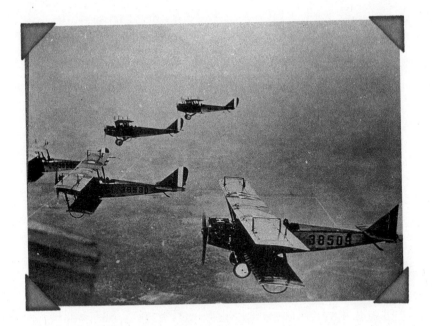

FLYING IN FORMATION.

up early, and Fritz's not stupid. He'll be waiting for us, so maintain discipline. Good luck."

We finish dressing and carry out a final check on our planes as the sky lightens to the east. The six Parasols rumble and bump along the grass runway and up into a glorious sunrise. Wispy clouds are painted dramatic shades of orange as the huge red disk of the sun hauls itself above the horizon and we climb toward our rendezvous. On magnificent mornings like this, I know I was born to fly.

Bowie and I set ourselves up in the formation that we used before, with me above and behind him. To the east, against the glare of the sun, I can just make out Jock and Mick flying line B. Wally is too far off to be seen.

Our progress is painfully slow, and if it weren't for the need for constant vigilance, it would be boring. Our 2c, far below, must fly slow and steady to get the photographs needed. I know that the pilot is working hard. The camera is a large wooden box attached to the side of the fuselage. While he's flying the plane, the pilot must lean out of his cockpit to take photographs at regular intervals while his observer keeps a lookout for the enemy. As I watch, I see small black clouds forming near the 2c. It looks strange in the clear sky, but I know that it's anti-aircraft fire from the trenches below—or Archie, as it is commonly called. The clouds look peaceful, but they're deadly if they get near their target. Fortunately, none form close to the 2c we're protecting.

Below us and slightly to the east, several black enemy observation balloons are performing the same function we are, looking hard for any changes behind our lines. Their crew has an easier job because the basket beneath the balloons is much steadier than our fragile aircraft. Their problem is that they can't run away if attacked.

Sooner or later, something will have to be done about the observation balloons. We all know that there is to be a big attack this summer, to help out the French, who are being hard pressed to the south at Verdun. I'm sure the Germans have worked out that there is an attack coming. What they don't yet know is where and when. If we can destroy the observation balloons, we will blind the enemy.

I become aware of Bowie waving to the east. Nervously, I scan the sky. There's the 2c of line B, photographing the reserve trenches, and there's the protection above, but there's only one Parasol. I scan and eventually see the second, far ahead and diving. I look ahead of the dive and see another dark shape in the skies. It's a German two-seater. Mick must have seen it and decided to go for his fifth kill. Wally won't be happy that he has been disobeyed.

I watch as the gap closes. It all happens in silence, like a moving picture show. The German eventually sees Mick and begins twisting and turning, but Mick stays with him. Eventually the two-seater goes into a shallow dive over the lines. It looks as if Mick finally has his kill.

I scan east. Three black shapes are dancing wildly where I last saw Jock. Another is closing in on the 2c. I watch, horrified, as Jock fights for his life. From this distance, I can't tell who is who. Eventually, one shape spirals down. For a moment I hope that Jock has got one of his attackers, but then the other two black shapes dive toward the observation plane, which is already twisting away from the third Fokker on his tail. The 2c dives hard for our lines, zigzagging from side to side. If he can keep ahead of his attackers, he has a chance. The 2c has a gun that can fire backward, discouraging straight attacks from above and behind.

Between scans of the otherwise empty sky, I watch the race for safety with fascination. It's hard not to go down and help, but I'll obey my orders. To my great relief, the enemy pilots break off the attack as our plane crosses the lines. Unfortunately, this leaves them free to go after our 2c.

I watch as the three Fokkers climb to get into position to attack. Then Bowie waves his arm and launches his Parasol into a steep dive. I follow. We have the advantage of height and hit the Fokkers while they are still climbing. Bowie goes in first, guns hammering, and the lead enemy plane bursts into flames and falls. Then it's an insanity of twirling, weaving, looping machines. I fire as shapes flash in front of me and pull away violently as I almost take the tail off one. I get behind one and empty my magazine to no visible effect.

The fight feels as if it lasts for hours, but it can be only a few minutes at most before the two remaining Fokkers break away and dive for home. I want to follow, but there's little I can do until I've changed magazines on my Lewis gun, and in any case, Bowie waves me back into position above the 2c, who has calmly continued his work as the fight raged around him.

I reload my Lewis gun. This is not easy. It involves standing up on the cockpit, holding the stick between my knees, leaning forward and replacing the round magazine on top of the gun. Not something I would enjoy doing in the middle of a dogfight! There are no further incidents as our two-seater finishes its run, and with relief, we turn for home. We escort our 2c back over the lines and wave at him as he turns for his landing strip to the south.

OPERATING THE LEWIS GUN FROM THE COCKPIT.

I have mixed feelings about our work. Two enemy planes have been destroyed, but we lost Jock and the B line was incomplete. I wonder what has happened to Wally's group, where Mick is and if the other 2c made it home.

My last question is answered as soon as we land. The 2c pilot headed for our airstrip, which is closer than his own, and now the plane sits at the end of our runway with a collapsed undercarriage. Fortunately, the pilot and observer are all right, with only a few scratches. Their plane has taken a lot of punishment, however, and there are several long tears in the fabric. Mick's plane is sitting outside the barn, but there is no sign of the pilot.

"Where's Mick?" I ask one of the fitters after I've removed the Pour le Mérite and climbed out.

"'E landed 'bout 'alf an 'our ago," the man says in a heavy Cockney accent. "Without so much as a by-your-leave, 'e jumps in the lorry and 'eads off down the road."

Bowie and I are busy cleaning the foul-smelling castor oil off our faces when we hear the sound of aeroplane engines. We rush outside, and I'm relieved to see two Parasols approach above the trees and land without incident. They were attacked by a single Fokker, Wally explains, but drove him off without too much trouble. Bowie and I describe to Wally what happened with us. He congratulates us on a job well done, then leads those around us in applause for Bowie's third kill. But he stresses that our greater achievement was allowing the observer in the 2c to do his job.

When we tell him about Mick his face clouds in anger, and when the pilot of the wrecked 2c says he completed only about half his run, Wally swears viciously under his breath.

"We're going to have to go out this afternoon and complete that run," he says. His voice is calm, but I can see from the set of his jaw and the cold look in his eyes how angry he is. "And that 2c is a write-off." He turns to me. "Did you see Jock go down? Did he manage to regain control?"

"I don't know," I reply. "He was still spinning when I lost sight of him."

"Let's hope he landed safely and is a prisoner. Where's Mick?"

As if in answer, the noise of a lorry fills the air. We watch as it turns in from the road and bumps to a halt in front of us. Mick jumps down, runs around to the other side and hauls a scared-looking German pilot out the passenger door. The German is pale and there's a large bloodstain on his right shoulder. He's holding his arm gingerly across his chest.

Mick pushes his prisoner forward, as if presenting a trophy. "He came down in a field five or six miles behind our front lines," he explains. "The machine's a write-off and the observer's had it, but I brought this fellow along for entertainment. Thought he should be with us when we celebrate tonight."

There's a strange, wild look in Mick's eyes. His enthusiasm is met with a stony silence.

Wally steps forward. "Do you have the slightest idea what you have done?" he asks, his voice dangerously quiet.

"I made my fifth kill," Mick answers, elation quickly turning to puzzlement.

"You disobeyed a direct order to stay with your 2c. As a result, the observation could not be completed, and someone is going to have to go out this afternoon and finish it. Jock, who obeyed orders and stayed at his post, was attacked by two Fokkers, and you were not there to help him. He went down behind the enemy lines and we can only pray that he survived to be taken prisoner.

"This squadron is a unit. We will only defeat the likes of Immelmann if we work together. I proved that when we were attacked, and so did Bowie and the Kid. Your lax discipline proved the opposite. I could have you court-martialed."

"Court-martialed?!" Mick steps forward and thrusts out his chin. "You wanted an ace for this squadron as much as I did. Now you've got one. What are we here for if not to kill the enemy? And I'm the best you've got at doing that. Every Fritz I shoot down is one less who can attack your precious 2cs. If you want babysitters, use these boys." Mick waves his arm to encompass everyone else. "I'm a hunter and I work alone." He pushes past Wally and the rest of us and stalks off.

We stand, silent and uncomfortable, as Wally stares after Mick. Then he turns back to the rest of us. "Put this man under guard and tend to his wounds," he orders, indicating the captured German pilot. "The rest of you clean up and fill out your flight reports." He looks at the fitters and riggers, who've been watching all this from a distance. "And I want all the planes serviced and refueled, and full damage reports on those that are in no condition to fly."

Wally heads off toward the radio tent, presumably to arrange a rendezvous with a 2c to complete the morning's work and to find someone to pick up the crew of the wrecked plane.

"Who's right?" I ask Bowie.

He shrugs. "Don't know, Kid. Maybe they both are. We certainly need to protect the reconnaissance boys, and one way to do that is to fly cover over them. Trouble is, we put two planes over each two-seater, Fritz attacks with three. We put three up, and he attacks with four. He has the advantage of fighting over his own territory, and until we have either overwhelming numbers or superior machines, it's going to be tough.

"The other approach is to send single machines out to hunt, the way Mick does, and hope they can intercept Fritz before he hits the two-seaters. Whichever approach is best, I sure hope they give us more planes and more pilots before this big attack that's coming."

Bowie wanders off deep in thought, leaving me thoroughly confused. Jock's missing and Mick is a cold-blooded killer who doesn't seem to care. This is nothing like the war I expected.

CHAPTER 13

A Visitor—May 1916

It's mid-afternoon in late May, and my fitter and I have been checking over my Parasol after the flight south to our new aerodrome near the town of Albert on the River Somme. It's a beautiful spring day and the birds are singing in the surrounding trees. Only the distant rumble of the guns reminds me how close we are to the fighting.

Just as I finish rubbing oil off my hands, I'm stunned to hear a familiar voice over my shoulder. "Here you are, Eddie Boy! I've caught up with you at last."

I spin round to see Alec smiling at me. He looks older than I remember, broader across the chest and suntanned, but the smile is the same. My first thought is that he got his transfer to the RFC, but then I notice that he's wearing a soldier's khaki uniform. "What are you doing here?"

"Now that's a nice welcome, I must say. I come all the way from Egypt to say hello and I don't even get a handshake."

"You surprised me, that's all," I say, grinning as we shake hands. "How did you find me?"

"No trouble," Alec says. "I just asked the first military policeman I met to point me toward the best Canadian pilot around. He said that there weren't any good Canadian pilots, but he'd heard there was a prairie kid who could jump really high." We laugh.

"And this is from someone who, by the looks of it"— I stare pointedly at Alec's uniform—"didn't even get into the RFC."

"True enough, Eddie," Alec acknowledges good-naturedly. "Turns out flying's not for me. Rather keep my feet on the ground—or *under* the ground, I should say."

"Underground?"

"Apparently someone looked at my application for a transfer and saw that I was a hard-rock miner. I'm called for an interview for what I think's the RFC, only to be met by an officer from the Royal Engineers. He sees how short I am and I'm down a damp tunnel under

no-man's-land faster than you can say Jack Robinson."
Alec laughs. "It's not too bad, though. The Newfoundland
boys're just up the road, so I still get to see my mates."
Alec looks over at the chateau where the pilots are bil-
leted. It was clearly a magnificent house in its day, but
now all the windows are blown out and there are patched
shell holes in the walls from the fighting in 1914.

"You going to invite me into your fancy new lodgings?
Or are they too good for your old friends?" Alec asks.

"They *are* too good for you, but I'm an influential
person round here. I'll get you in." We walk across the
grass toward the chateau. Seeing Alec again is like a
breath of fresh air. His joking banter harks back to happier days. Unfortunately, it also reminds me of Cecil.
"We just flew in here this morning," I say, pushing my
memories to the back of my mind.

"That's what I heard. I'm back to the line tonight,
so I thought I'd better drop over to see you this afternoon. Mind you"—Alec scans the runway, the camou-
flaged hangar for the planes and the wooden sheds
where the mechanics work—"looks as if the place was
ready for you."

"We pilots are too important to have to work," I say
with a smile.

Just then, a particularly loud rumble breaks the
silence.

"That's one of those big howitzers," Alec observes. "Fires a shell the size of a small cow almost straight up in the air. Comes down on Fritz out of nowhere. Makes a hole you could build a house in. Wouldn't like to be under one. Still, I'll be safe enough deep underground."

"You reckon this is where the big attack's going to happen?"

"I don't doubt it for a minute," Alec says. "You haven't been here for a night yet. You won't get a minute's sleep. The roads are crazy from dusk to dawn—lorries, tractors, marching feet—and they've built miles of railway

A HOWITZER CANNON.

lines as well. You won't believe the stuff that's being brought up: guns, ammo, duckboards, sandbags. And it's all got to be hidden somewhere. I reckon your job, Eddie Boy, will be to stop Fritz flying over to take too close a look."

"And what's your job, Alec?"

"Same as always—digging holes." A serious look forms on Alec's face. "I'll tell you, though. Come the battle, there's going to be large bits of the Hun trenches that won't exist anymore."

That's all I can get out of him. We go into the chateau and find ourselves a couple of chairs in what used to be a magnificent parlor. The floor-to-ceiling fireplace is still there, and a vast, dusty crystal chandelier hangs from the center of the ceiling. Alec tells me a few stories about his time in Egypt, but he seems more interested in what I've been up to.

I find that talking is a relief. I can say things to Alec that I can't say in my letters home, even if the censors would allow it. I give him more details about Cecil's death, about Wally and Bowie, and about what happened that day with Mick and Jock.

"Mick went off on leave and Wally didn't court-martial him," I relate. "We didn't know what had happened to Jock for two weeks, but we all hoped he was a prisoner. One morning, just as the sun was thinking about coming up, we heard a strange plane overhead. It was a German two-seater and we all thought it was a bombing attack. The pilot swooped low over the airstrip and we all dove for shelter, but the only thing he dropped was a canvas bag on the end of a crude parachute. When we opened it, we found Jock's personal effects and his bagpipes, along with a note."

I rummage in my pocket. No one seemed to know what to do with the note, so I kept it. I read it to Alec.

English Flyers,

We are returning the effects of the brave pilot who fell behind our lines on April 1. Although outnumbered, he fought well and did not run. We found him dead in his crashed machine and buried him with full military honors.

We are sorry for your loss.

Your comrades in the sky

"It was just as well that Mick was away on leave," I add.

"Chivalry among the knights of the air," Alec says. I detect a bitter tone to his voice. "You ever been in the trenches?" he asks.

"No," I admit. "I've only seen them from a couple of thousand feet up."

"I reckon the smell doesn't get that high. Not much time for chivalry down there. Best those poor blighters can hope for is a few hours of sleep in a hole in the ground and a warm meal once in a while. Even a burrowing mole like me has a better life than they do, even on a quiet section of the line. But listen to me moaning on! You obviously survived. You an ace yet?"

I laugh. "Five doesn't sound like a lot, but it's hard to get. The weeks before we moved here were quiet. Most of the German planes are down fighting the French at Verdun, so the patrols weren't dangerous. Wally got his fourth at the end of April, so he's our closest to an ace until Mick returns. I got number two, a two-seater reconnaissance craft that spun and then dove away, but I won't be credited with it. No one saw it crash so there's no official confirmation and I still sit on one."

"You've just got to work harder, Eddie Boy," Alec says with a smile.

"Maybe," I acknowledge. "But if you get too focused on getting kills, it distorts your thinking. You end up like Mick. We have to remember that the only reason we're up there is to protect the work the observers do." I look at my friend, serious now. "They say the two most dangerous times for a pilot are the first few weeks and after he's been flying for months. We lost a couple of new pilots who hadn't been with the squadron long. I can't even remember what they looked like. It's best not to make friends with the new pilots too quickly." I laugh bitterly. "I guess I'm getting to be a heartless old veteran." Talking about all this to Alec is bringing out feelings I've kept buried for weeks. I don't like them.

"Do you still feel the same way about flying that you did on the boat over here? You really got *me* fired up about it back then."

"I don't know," I say after some thought. "Sometimes, at dawn or sunset, when the clouds look like a wonderful painting in some great art gallery, I can recapture the feelings I had flying across the prairies with Uncle Horst or Ted. But mostly I'm over the lines and scanning everywhere for a dark shape swooping at me out of the sun or the black puffs of Archie edging closer."

"You've got a future as a poet," Alec says.

I laugh. "I don't think so. At the end of a day of patrols, even if there's been no fighting, I crawl into my bunk, so exhausted that I sleep like the dead. Funny thing is, I wake just as tired as I was when I went to bed."

"Yeah," Alec agrees. "I feel exactly the same after a day of digging in a tunnel. It's the not knowing. Is there a Hun camouflet—that's one of their counter tunnels—ready to blow a few feet away? It must be much the same knowing there's a Hun plane you can't see ready to jump you."

"I guess that's it. The worst thing, though, is when you see an enemy pilot's face. Most of the time you can pretend it's a game and convince yourself that the plane you're hunting is just an inanimate object. Then you get close and see the look of terror on a man's face, and you realize that you're busily trying to kill someone."

"How're things at home?" Alec asks, changing the subject.

"Fine," I say. "Mom writes most weeks. It's good to hear that everyone's all right, but it's hard to care about the mundane things she talks about."

"Yeah," Alec concurs. "I almost dread those letters from home. No one there understands what our world's like."

"I know what you mean," I say. "My uncle Horst sent me a letter all about building his new flying machine in his barn. Once upon a time, Horst's planes were the most important things in my life. Now they're machines I use to try to kill people."

"It's a funny old war right enough." Alec stands up and stretches. "Well, I'd better be off if I don't want to be left behind. I'd invite you to visit, Eddie, but there's not much room in the tunnels. I'll try to drop by again next time I'm out of the line."

"It was good to see you," I say, accompanying Alec outside. "Look after yourself."

"You too."

We shake hands and I watch Alec head out to the road. Odd how we have ended up, me high in the sky and him deep underground—the top and bottom of the war. I head back into the chateau. Tomorrow we go on our first reconnaissance flight to familiarize ourselves with the new sector of the front, and I have maps to examine before that. I suspect this new airfield is going to be much busier than I'm used to.

CHAPTER 14

Shot Down—June 1916

I am right about things being busy on this sector of the front. It seems that every day there's a dogfight. The troubling thing is that as the days pass, the German presence increases. Day by day there are more patrols looking for us and more planes in each patrol. For a while we're lucky—a few wounded pilots and several planes limping home with damage, but no one's lost and we're commended on our work protecting the observers. Then we're given a special mission.

"I've got something different for you this morning," says Wally, having gathered us round the big table under the chandelier in the chateau's parlor. The table is covered with maps, and Wally is explaining the morning's patrols. He has already assigned tasks to most of the pilots, but Bowie and I are wondering what he has in store for us.

"As you know," Wally says, "Fritz has fortified the villages behind his front line. We know about Beaumont-Hamel—we've photographed every square inch of it a hundred times."

There's a grumble of agreement from the pilots, and my stomach knots. I've been over Beaumont-Hamel. It's low-level work and dangerous. There's not only the regular Archie, but the Germans also have modified machine guns that are a problem when flying close to the ground. No one wants to go back there.

"And we've done the same to the Hawthorn Redoubt in front of it," Wally continues. "What we don't yet know is what the infantry's going to be facing after the Hun front lines are broken. Have they fortified the villages behind the front? And if so, how well? You three"—he gestures to me, Bowie and a new pilot called Gordon—"have the job of escorting a two-seater to photograph the village behind Beaumont-Hamel." Wally runs his finger over the map. "Beaucourt-sur-l'Ancre. Should be a piece of cake. Just follow the railway running beside the river and there you are. You don't even have to fly over Beaumont-Hamel."

I feel a sense of relief, but it doesn't last long.

"Thing is, HQ wants the pictures taken from a thousand feet."

"A thousand feet!" both Bowie and I exclaim at the same time. "They could hit us with rocks at that height."

Wally shrugs. There's nothing he can do. Orders are orders. "With luck, coming along the river, Fritz won't be expecting you, so you'll get in and out before he can react."

"That's a lot of luck," Bowie cries. "Still, you can't live forever, eh, Kid? Come on Gordo," he says, giving the new pilot an instant nickname. "Let's go and make sure everything's working on the old Parasols."

I touch the Pour le Mérite in my pocket. I have a feeling I'll need it.

Bowie and I help Gordo run over the checklist before takeoff and stress the factors he needs to remember in flying the touchy Parasol. He's a nice kid and the best of the new additions, with almost twenty hours' experience, some of it on Parasols, but I'm short with him. I don't want him to be my friend because his chances of being alive in a few weeks are not good.

"Why did Wally give us him?" I ask Bowie as we head toward our machines, annoyed that we don't have a more experienced companion.

"Who else's he going to send?" Bowie replies. "There aren't enough pilots with enough training, and there aren't enough good machines. Maybe if Fritz goes for him, it'll give us a better chance."

What Bowie says is cynical, but if I'm honest, that thought has occurred to me too. I shake my head. "Is this what we've come to—hoping that the inexperienced boy we're being sent up with will be killed because it'll give us a better chance to live?"

"Hey," Bowie says, grabbing my arm, "don't start thinking about him. He'll take his chances like the rest of us did when we first arrived. You start babysitting him and you'll be distracted. That means you'll be the one to go down. Keep focused on the work."

I nod, pull on my helmet and goggles, clamber into the cockpit and wrap Horst's medal around a spar. I stare at it for a long moment. Max Immelmann was awarded one of these back in January when he shot down his eighth Allied aircraft. How can something that is given as an honor to my enemies be my lucky charm? I shake my head to dispel these negative thoughts. My medal was a gift from Horst, and that's what makes it lucky. I have to believe that.

We take off without incident, rendezvous with the B.E.2c we are to protect and cross the front lines. They're on us almost instantly—four Fokkers, two coming in from each side. We're flying in a V above the 2c, but they ignore us and dive straight for the two-seater. Bowie veers off at the two attackers on the right, signaling for Gordo and me to go for the other two. I wave for Gordo to follow me and push the stick forward.

Almost immediately, I'm in the middle of the swirling, chaotic mess of a dogfight. I get off a few shots at one Fokker, but the pilot's good and flashes out of my line of sight. I turn toward the other and fire, but this time I'm too far away. I scan the sky quickly and climb to gain height for another attack.

Bowie's off to the south, curving and turning in a deadly dance with the other two Fokkers. At least we're keeping the enemy planes away from our 2c. I look in the other direction and see Gordo flying in a straight line, absolute insanity in a dogfight. Sure enough, one of the Fokkers is diving onto his tail. I bank and dive after him. The Fokker pilot's holding his fire until he's close enough to be sure of the kill. Maybe I have enough time.

I'm near enough to see Gordo turn his head just as the Fokker opens fire. The Parasol jerks as if kicked by an invisible foot. Red flames leap out of the fuselage, engulfing the cockpit. The wing folds, and the fiery ball of man and machine plummets to the ground. In a hopeless rage, I let off a long burst at the Fokker, to no obvious effect. I'm so angry that I forget to scan and don't see the second Fokker until I feel a sharp pain in my right thigh and see bullets tear into my engine. Hot oil sprays back over me as I throw my fragile plane left and right, trying to shake off my attacker.

I'm too low to go into a deliberate spin, so my only hope is to dive. As my engine dies, I throw the stick forward; the nose drops sickeningly and the ground rushes up at me. I guess my sudden maneuver at least fools the German pilot—or he assumes I'm dead. Either way, he flashes past above me and dives away toward the 2c.

I don't care what he does. My priority is to avoid burying myself and the Parasol in the ground. I haul back on the stick with all my strength, praying that the wings don't rip off with the force. With terrifying slowness, the nose rises and my speed drops. I'm barely two hundred feet above the ground when I level out, but I'm losing height all the time. It's eerily quiet without the roar of the engine. I hope I'm headed in the right direction and have enough height and speed to clear the lines and get down on our side. It doesn't look good.

I lose more precious speed avoiding a small copse of trees, then I'm above the trenches. Startled faces look up only a few feet below me. They're German, but everyone is too surprised to open fire. Someone even waves at me. Then I'm over the wire. The ground looks green and peaceful, like one of Horst's fields. The only clues that I am not at home are the lack of animals and the occasional brown crater made by a heavy shell.

I can see the British wire ahead of me, but I don't have enough height to get over it. I concentrate on putting the Parasol down before she stalls and I drop like a stone. I narrowly miss a solitary, branchless tree before I bump hard and the undercarriage gives way. The Parasol slews wildly to one side and slides into the dense wire.

For what seems an age—as I sit shaking with the relief at still being alive—there is silence. Then a machine gun chatters, slow and heavy like my mom's treadle sewing machine.

"Are you still alive?" a voice shouts from the trench in front of me.

"Yes," I shout back.

"Well, you won't be for long if you don't get out of there and over here." As if to emphasize the point, a line of holes appear in the Parasol's wing. I rip my harness off and haul myself out. But when I try to run, my right leg gives way beneath me and I collapse onto the grass, strands of barbed wire snagging at my jacket.

"Keep your head down and crawl left," the hidden voice advises.

By now there's rifle and machine-gun fire from both sides, and I can hear bullets whining over me.

The Pour le Mérite! I forgot it. It's still tied in the cockpit. I turn my head, but the bullets snapping through the Parasol convince me that it would be suicide to try to get back to the plane, even if I could make it with my injured leg. My lucky charm will have to wait until later.

Lying on my left side to minimize the pain, I slither along until I come to a break in the wire. I crawl through and fall, with great relief and a shout of pain, onto the fire step inside the trench.

My leg is in agony. I look down to see a long tear in my trouser on the outside of my thigh and a spreading bloodstain. I feel weak and nauseous. But at least the machine-gun fire is dying down.

"You're lucky, flyboy." I look up to see an officer standing before me. He's wearing the distinctive blue puttees of the Newfoundland Regiment, and there's a lance corporal standing behind him. "Second Lieutenant Jim Raleigh," he says, holding out his hand. "Welcome to our little corner of paradise. Thought you were headed for the Danger Tree out there. You didn't miss it by much. I'll get my servant, Lance Corporal Broughton, to take a look at that leg."

We shake hands and I introduce myself. Then Broughton steps forward, cuts open my trouser leg and begins washing the wound. I clench my teeth.

"Looks like you're in for a rest, sir," he says cheerfully. "Maybe even some home leave. Doesn't look too bad, though. Deep, but I can't see any bone. Keep it clean and let those lovely nurses fuss over you, and you'll be right as rain in a couple of weeks."

"Thank you," I say as he begins wrapping a bandage tightly around my thigh.

"I've seen lots worse," Broughton declares. "I used to be an orderly in the hospital in St. John's. The wounds I've seen on those fisherman and sealers coming back to port, you wouldn't believe."

I'm feeling a bit better, and as Broughton chatters on, I look around. Everything I see makes me glad to be a pilot. The trench is deep enough to stand in and the wall I'm leaning against is sandbagged, but the rest is muddy. Pieces of equipment are scattered all over, and men are sprawled either on the fire step or in shallow holes dug out of the trench wall. There's a strong smell of earth and nearby toilets, but there's also something else, a strange sweetness that underlies the heavier odors.

"Not the clean air you're used to, I bet," says Raleigh, appearing to read my mind. "We took this stretch over

SOLDIERS IN THE TRENCHES SURROUNDED BY SANDBAGS.

from the French. There's not been much fighting here recently, but occasionally an exploding shell turns up a body from the early days. Not pleasant, but what can you do? Can you walk?"

"I don't know," I say.

"You sit there for a minute, sir," says Broughton, tying off the ends of the bandage. "I've got just the thing for you. There's a pile of broken duckboards down the communication trench. There's a bit there that'd be just right. Not the perfect crutch, but it'll do for now." He stands and hurries off.

"When you're set, come along to the dugout and we can work out how to get you back to your unit." Raleigh retreats along the trench and ducks into an opening on the right.

The lance corporal returns with a length of wood from one of the duckboards that line the bottom of the trench. There are several crosspieces attached. He breaks off all but one that's about the right height for me to grip if I place the wood under my armpit. With his help and encouragement, I stand up and try my weight on the crutch. It works well.

"Thank you," I say. My leg hurts, but the bandage helps a lot and I can hobble about. I make my way down to Raleigh's dugout and duck past the gas curtain. The room I enter is larger than I expected, although the usable space is cut down by the wood pillars that support the ceiling beams. The floor is covered with duckboards, but the walls are damp mud. To my left is a crude wooden bunk with an earthenware rum jar propped at one end. Ahead is a desk cluttered with maps and the stubs of candles. A small shelf above holds an oil lamp, a tin mug, several bottles and a copy of *Alice's Adventures in Wonderland*. To my right is an alcove with a radio on a small table. Equipment, items of uniforms and assorted weapons hang from nails driven into the support pillars. It's a far cry from the parlor in the chateau, with its fireplace and chandelier.

"Come in, come in. Have a seat." Raleigh waves vaguely toward the desk. He's leaning over the radio, talking into the mouthpiece. I prop my makeshift crutch against the wall and sit gingerly on a chair. When Raleigh finishes, he takes a second chair. "Well, there's a lorry coming to pick you up at the dressing station, but you'll need to walk that far, I'm afraid."

"I'll manage," I say.

"They can check your wound at the dressing station and tell you where you need to go from there. Meanwhile, I'll have Broughton make us some tea."

As if on cue, Broughton ducks into the dugout carrying a tray with a teapot and two mugs on it.

"The man's a wonder," Raleigh says. "Always one step ahead of me."

"Cup of tea never goes amiss, sir," Broughton says, putting down the tray. "Sorry I couldn't rustle up any milk."

"That's fine, Broughton. Thank you."

While the tea's being poured, I ask, "You're the Newfoundland Regiment?"

"Indeed," Raleigh confirms. "You're familiar with that part of the world?"

"I'm Canadian," I reply. "From Saskatchewan, but I know someone who was in the regiment—Alec Hamilton."

"Ah, yes. He joined us after Egypt. Wanted to become pilot, I recall, but they sent him underground. He's nearby, I'm told, working on the mine up the line."

"I know. He visited when my squadron first arrived here."

"Let's hope what he's doing helps."

"The big attack's coming soon?"

"Twenty-ninth of the month, I hear, but it's supposed to be a secret. Word is, the artillery barrage beforehand will be the biggest of the war. With that and the mines, it's supposed to be a breeze. All the infantry will have to do is walk over what's left of the Hun trenches. I hope so. Fritz does seem to be well dug in over there."

"Think it'll end the war?"

"If it does, the Newfoundlanders will be a big part of it. We're not in the first wave, but after the German lines are taken, we push through. I must say, it'll be good to get out into open country. As you can see, life in these trenches is a little confining."

"I was protecting some photo reconnaissance of Fritz's rear area, Beaucourt-sur-l'Ancre, when I was hit."

"That's good. We'll need those maps when we get going. Speaking of which, you should probably head off if you're going to meet that lorry. Broughton can show you the way. And I'll send some boys through the wire tonight to salvage what we can from your plane. I imagine Fritz's had a good few shots at it, but we should get the Lewis gun."

"If I can ask a favor," I say. "I have a medal, a blue cross, that I take up with me in the cockpit for luck. In my rush to get out, I forgot it. Could you ask whoever goes out to fetch it and send it on to the squadron?"

"Certainly. We need all the luck we can get out here."

We both stand, shake hands and wish each other good fortune in the coming battle.

Broughton helps me along the cluttered communication trench and out into the wider reserve trench.

"We call this one St. John's Road because it's the way home," he tells me.

Fortunately it's not far to the dressing station and the lorry's already there waiting for me. I say my goodbyes and thanks to Broughton. A doctor takes a cursory look at my wound, compliments the job done on it and tells me there's nothing more he can do. He gives me a chit for the reserve hospital outside Amiens and tells me that there are no ambulances, so the lorry's probably my best way to get there.

I persuade the lorry driver to stop off at the squadron, where I learn that while Bowie returned safely, the

B.E.2c was shot down after Gordo. Everyone wishes me well and I set off for Amiens, in agony at every bump in the road, but worried most of all that I've lost Horst's Pour le Mérite.

CHAPTER 15

Preparing—June 1916

My last hope for retrieving Horst's Pour le Mérite is crushed when I arrive back at the chateau after my short spell in hospital at Amiens. I'm excited when Wally tells me something was delivered from the Newfoundlanders while I was away, but it's only a scrawled note from Lieutenant Raleigh.

I hope your wound has healed, but I'm afraid I have some bad news. After you left with Broughton, Fritz targeted your plane relentlessly with machine-gun fire and trench mortars. Just before evening stand-to, they hit it square on and started a fire. All we could do was watch as it burned. I sent a patrol out that night, but they could salvage little. They brought back the Lewis gun, although it was in bad shape. Perhaps we can rescue some parts. As you requested, I had the patrol search for your medal. Unfortunately, there was no sign of it. The fire was hottest around the cockpit, and there was little left that was recognizable. Even if your medal survived and was missed in the dark, it must have been badly damaged by the fire. I am truly sorry we could not find it. I know how important these things are.

We are out of the line at present, but we'll return in a few days for the big attack. I wish you well and all luck in the upcoming affair.

Again, my apologies.

Jim Raleigh

I feel like I have failed Horst. He entrusted me with this important family heirloom and I allowed it to be destroyed. Why didn't I take the medal out of the cockpit with me? I know the answer to that—if I had stayed to untangle the Pour le Mérite, I would probably be dead now. But I'm filled with conflicting emotions. On the one hand, the medal didn't seem to bring me luck on my last flight. I was, after all, wounded and shot down. On the other hand, I survived and managed to get home. Maybe I stopped believing in my lucky charm when I heard that Max Immelmann had been awarded one. But still, I can't help wondering where my luck will come from now.

"Did you hear?" I turn to see Wally standing in the doorway. "Immelmann's gone. He was shot down and killed near Lenz a few days back." I guess I look more miserable than I should, because Wally goes on to say, "You don't look too happy to hear the news."

"I'm glad we won't have to worry about Immelmann anymore," I say, trying to force a smile, "but I've lost my lucky charm. It's silly, but I feel miserable without it."

"It's not silly," Wally says. "This war isn't rational and we have no control over our fate. Archie explodes below you, an engine fails at three thousand feet, a wing folds in a dive, a Fokker comes at you out of the sun—there's a hundred things that can kill you and sometimes luck's all that keeps us alive."

"And I've lost mine."

"No, you haven't. Luck's up here." Wally taps his temple. "The charms are just what we link the luck to. When Jock's luck ran out, having his bagpipes in the cockpit didn't help him."

"I suppose you're right. I've never seen you with a good luck charm."

Wally looks a bit sheepish. "I have one, but it's much sillier than yours." He lowers his voice to a whisper. "I sing."

"Sing? What do you sing?"

"Do you know that music hall artist who died last year, Billy Williams?"

"The Man in the Velvet Suit?"

"That's him. My mom and dad took me to see him once at the Oxford Music Hall. It was a bit lower class for our family, and I think Mom was quite uncomfortable, even in one of the balcony boxes, but I adored every minute of it. Williams was my favorite and I learned every one of his songs: 'When Father Papered the Parlour,' 'I Wish It Was Sunday Night,' 'There's Life in the Old Dog Yet.' If I sing one of them as I take off, I know I'll be fine. And you thought taking a medal with you was eccentric!"

We both laugh. The image of Wally singing music hall songs makes me feel better.

"So your wound wasn't bad enough for a spell in England?" Wally asked.

"It might have been. My thigh became infected and I ran a high fever for a few days. It still hurts, actually, but I asked to come back here and they were only too happy to oblige with the big attack coming."

"I'm touched that you missed us," Wally says with a smile. "You'll see a few new faces, but all the old hands are still here. Bowie got two in one day, so he's our second ace. Mind, they wouldn't give him leave because of the attack."

"Second ace?"

"Yes. Mick's back." I must look surprised, because Wally adds, "I didn't court-martial him or report him. We need all the good flyers we can get, and he is the best we've got at killing Fritz. He's bagged another two since he returned. I can't control him, and maybe I shouldn't try. He flies alone and all I do is tell him which direction to go."

"Is he all right?" I ask, remembering his anger and his obsession with getting his fifth kill.

"To be honest, he worries me a bit. You know Mick— he's always been a bit of a loner, likes to keep himself to himself. I don't mind that so much—we all do what we must to handle this business—but the last Fritz he shot down has changed him."

"How so?"

"It was a Fokker. The pilot didn't see Mick until he was right on him. First burst hit the gas tank, and the Fokker flamed. Mick followed him down to make sure. Now, he's never said what happened, but I think he watched the pilot burn to death on the way down. In any case, Mick's carried a revolver with him in the cockpit ever since. I don't think he plans to burn."

We stand in silence for a minute, thinking. It's always dreadful, watching someone go down. It takes a long time to fall from five thousand feet and pilots are often aware of what awaits them, but fire is a particular horror.

I try to change the subject. "You haven't got your fifth yet?"

"I don't get to fly too much these days. Always off at some conference learning what we're supposed to do in the coming attack. Speaking of which, it's been postponed."

"I heard it was scheduled for tomorrow, June 29."

"That was the plan. Five days of intense bombardment, then the attack. But the weather's not cooperating, so it's July 1 now. Gives us more time to see if the artillery's done its job—destroyed Fritz's guns, collapsed his trenches and cut the wire. That's what you'll be doing tomorrow: escorting reconnaissance planes photographing the damage we've managed to do to Fritz's guns. I think we've got most of them. There's certainly not much return fire coming over these days."

"Sounds like the same old routine," I say.

"Not quite. We put four Parasols up now to cover a two-seater. It gives us and the observer more protection. Fritz's not pushing us too hard at the moment, but that'll change as soon as the attack goes in. The main danger at the moment's being hit by our own shells. It's the strangest thing. You're up there, thousands of feet in the air, and you can see these big howitzer shells turning as they reach the top of their arc and begin to go down. You can follow them for a long way. Of course they'd make a mess of a machine if they hit you. Even the turbulence if you're too close can tear off a wing.

"But our role will change as well as soon as the attack starts. When the infantry goes over the top, we go down to support them. A whole system of signals has been worked out, and it'll be our job to recognize those signals and let HQ know how far units have advanced so we don't shell our own men. We'll also do ground attack at targets of opportunity. Say you see Fritz massing for a counterattack. A few well-placed bursts from the Lewis gun might just discourage him. We've also received some small bombs that we can take up and drop by hand. We all have to play our part to make this thing a success and end the war."

I'm pondering what Wally's said when I'm interrupted by a loud thunk. It startles me, but I know just where the knife sticking into the wall comes from.

"Hi, Bowie," I say, turning. "I see you still can't hit anything with those things."

"I can hit something if I want to. How you doing, Kid?"

"I'm doing well. I hear you're an exalted ace now."

"Yeah, but I still got to hang out with the likes of you. If I'd known that, I wouldn't have tried so hard to be a hero."

"Or spent so much energy telling everyone what a hero you are," Wally says.

"You're just jealous," Bowie responds. "Come on, Kid. I'll introduce you to the new faces."

The parlor is filled with pilots waiting for dinner to be called. I recognize a few of the faces, but many are new to me. They all look very young, which is odd, because many of them are older than me. I suppose it's because they haven't yet acquired the tired look around the eyes that marks those of us who have been here longest.

There's a forced cheerfulness to the room as everyone works at getting rid of the tension from the day and tries not to think about tomorrow. Only Mick, alone in a corner cleaning his service revolver, is silent. I go over and say hello. Mick looks up and nods, but goes on with his obsessive cleaning. I turn away, trying not to think what it must be like falling from the sky in a burning plane. Perhaps Mick's revolver makes more sense than bagpipes or an old medal.

The reconnaissance patrols on June 29 and 30 are not much use, and we lose one of the new pilots. One of his wings folds while he's over the front lines. Whether it was thanks to one of our shells or simply a structural failure, I don't suppose we'll ever know. He never stood a chance.

There's low cloud most of the two days. Even when we go up, we can see very little through the fog that blankets much of the ground. We do the best we can, but I don't know how useful our work is. Everyone is tense with anticipation. It's not helped by a lack of sleep. Every night is a racket of lorries and marching feet. Add to that the sound of the guns. We can hear the barrage above the noise of our engines, and they say it can be heard as a low rumbling as far away as London. I almost pity the German soldiers beneath it. Surely there can't be much left of their defenses after this.

On the afternoon of June 30, the clouds and fog finally clear and we get busy with final tasks. As we return to base, the lowering sun paints the landscape a gentle orange. It almost looks beautiful, the green countryside dotted with small farms and cut by straight roads and the zigzag lines of the trenches. Even the explosions—the white puffs of shrapnel bursts and darker columns rising from the earth where high explosives detonate—look magnificent from thousands of feet above.

I wonder what Alec is doing. His mining work must be finished by now, so has he been moved elsewhere or does he get to stay and watch the result of his labors? And what about Lieutenant Raleigh and Broughton? Are they ready for tomorrow? I decide to fly over the piece of no-man's-land where I crashed. I tell myself it's because that's where I'll be tomorrow, spotting signs of our advance, but really I'm just curious. I signal to Bowie and dive away.

It's easy to find the spot. Beaumont-Hamel stands out, and there is a distinctive Y-shaped ravine as part of the German front lines. I can even see the lone tree I almost hit, the Danger Tree, but there's no sign of the remains of my plane.

I'm surprised by how unscarred the land looks. After a week's intense bombardment, I had expected to see total devastation, but there is still grass on the ground and leaves on many of the trees. Of course, there are also many round shell holes, and new ones being created as I watch, but between the brown craters, the ground looks almost peaceful. What I find more disturbing is the state of the German trenches. They are collapsed in many places from direct hits, but long stretches look in frighteningly good shape. What scares me most is that the German wire still seems to be intact. I tell myself that the last part of the barrage tomorrow morning is probably designed to destroy the wire so the Germans won't have time to rebuild it before the advance. Since there has been virtually no return fire from the German artillery, I'm certain the first waves will have a fairly easy time of it.

Our trenches, both front line and reserve, are busy with troops, many eating around small fires. Several wave as I zoom low overhead. "Good luck tomorrow!" I shout, although there's no way they can hear me.

CHAPTER 16

The Attack—July 1, 1916

I don't think I would have slept much last night even if there had been no artillery barrage or traffic on the road. The tension is too much. Are we about to take part in the beginning of the end of the war? I think everyone feels the same, as we are all up before dawn, drinking coffee and checking over our equipment. By 5 a.m. the sun is crawling above the horizon and we are out inspecting our planes, making sure the guns are loaded and deciding how many of the twenty-pound bombs we can carry. It's unnecessary, of course—the fitters and riggers are as tense as we are, and they've made sure everything is ready.

"This morning we will not be escorting reconnaissance craft," Wally intones. He has gathered us round the table beneath the chandelier in the parlor. We went over everything last night—examining maps, familiarizing ourselves with our piece of the front line and learning the signals we can expect to see from the advancing troops—but it won't hurt to go over it once more. "We are to carry out contact patrols and attack targets of opportunity. On the ground, that's any concentration of enemy troops, supply convoys or trains, either moving or stationary; in the air, that's any enemy craft, regardless of number. The philosophy is 'Attack everything.' We must do our utmost to support the troops on the ground and make this attack a success.

"Our responsibility will be the 29th Division front line, from the Ancre river to Beaumont-Hamel. Most of you should know it like the back of your hand by now. The attack will begin all along the front at 7:30 a.m., and in our sector it will be signaled by the explosion of the mine beneath the Hawthorn Redoubt." Wally looks at me. "Let's hope your friend from Newfoundland did a good job. The mine's huge. It'll blow a big hole in the German lines, but it'll also throw a lot of stuff up in the air, and the shock wave will spread a long way. You'll need to be careful. The shock wave could rip your machine apart."

Wally waits for nods all around before he continues. "We take off at 7 a.m. Go above five thousand feet and get your bearings. When you see the mine go up, that signals the attack. Drop to between five hundred and a thousand feet so you can see what's going on. After that, use your discretion. Your primary role is to watch for the signals from the troops on the ground. The first waves have been given red flares, but I've heard that they don't want to use them because they will give away their position to Fritz, so watch for anything that might be a signal. Most units will have ground sheets to lay out, but watch for equipment arranged to form the division or battalion number. If you're not sure, go low enough to recognize the uniforms.

"When you see something—and you're sure of it—mark what you see on your map, put the map in the weighted bag, fly back to infantry headquarters and drop the bag. If for some reason you can't drop the bag, head back here and I'll radio the report in. Clear?"

"You're not flying today, Wally?" Bowie asks.

"Unfortunately not. Someone has to stay here and coordinate you lot. And one last thing: keep an eye on your time. You will use more fuel than you expect at low altitude, so don't run out. Good luck."

We're all ready well before 7 a.m., and Wally lets us go up on the understanding that we stay high until the attack starts. As I rise into the perfect blue summer sky, I have a feeling I've rarely had in all the bustle and chaos of the war. Despite the shells thundering past as the final bombardment reaches a crescendo, it's peaceful. This is how I felt that first day so long ago, when I went up solo above Horst's farm. It reminds me how much I love flying. I adore the sense of freedom up here in the clean air, far above the petty chaos that we puny humans make of the world below. What will I do if the optimists are right and the battle that's about to begin ends this war? I'll keep flying somehow. Horst is right— flying will change the world, and I want desperately to be a part of that. I wonder if it will be hard to go back to just flying? I think of the friends I've lost—Cecil, Jock and even the newcomers, like Gordo. We've shared things that no one who hasn't been through this can understand. Will I ever make friends like them again? Will I miss the life I am leading now? I shake my head before I drift into a dangerous distracted reverie. I have work to do.

I glance at my watch. It's 7:05. I scan the sky around me in quadrants. I can see Bowie to my south and slightly above, and Mick to the north. Others are scattered farther away, waiting. I can see no sign of any Fokkers. Are they here? I look to the east and the rising sun. Are they waiting for the battle to begin as well?

Above the clouds.

I look down. Five thousand feet below is Beaumont-Hamel, and somewhere underneath it is Alec's mine. The German trenches are invisible beneath the smoke and debris from the continually exploding shells. There can't be much left of the trenches or the defenders. It's going to be a great victory.

I can see our lines clearly. They look peaceful, but I know they are crammed to overflowing with the first wave of soldiers waiting to go over the top. I want to go lower to get a better look. My watch says 7:10, which is still twenty minutes before the attack. Plenty of time to go down and come back up again. I ease the Parasol into a gentle descending spiral.

At two thousand feet, I level out. From this height, the bombardment of the German trenches appears less intense. I can see individual explosions, as well as shrapnel in the air and gouts of earth where the high explosives embed themselves in the ground before detonating. The air is vibrating and there is a constant thunder. I strain to see what state the German defenses are in. Much of their front line has been reduced to a jumble of shell holes. The barbed wire still looks disturbingly intact, but there are large gaps and the lack of activity in the German trenches suggests that opposition will be light.

I look at my watch—7:15. I swing over Beaumont-Hamel for a final glimpse before I head back up to five thousand feet. The village has been heavily shelled, and several of the buildings are ruined. Trenches around it are still recognizable but deserted. Time to head back up. As I take one last glance, a patch of ground in front of the village appears to bulge up toward me. With fascinating slowness, the bulge explodes into a mass of dirt and rock that expands impossibly high, hesitates for a moment and then falls back to the earth. The column of dirt doesn't reach me, but the shock wave throws the Parasol to one side as if it's a dry leaf in a fall breeze.

I fight for control of the bucking plane. Luckily, the explosion has thrown me up, so I have some altitude to work with. Eventually, I'm back in charge and flying level. I look at my watch. It's only 7:23. The attack's not supposed to start for another ten minutes. I scan around. I'm some distance behind the front line. I can see German trenches, but they're the reserve lines. Behind me the artillery bombardment still engulfs the front lines.

As I begin to climb, the engine sounds rough and misfires a couple of times. I slow my climb to a series of gentle spirals. I'm almost back at five thousand feet when the Fokkers attack. There are four of them, coming from high and to the east. They have the advantage of position and speed. If I try to run, especially with a dodgy engine, I'm dead. I turn and fly straight at the lead plane.

With a combined speed of over one hundred miles an hour, we close quickly. I can see the flashes from his gun, but he's firing too early and, head on, I'm a small target—I hope. The trick is to keep my nerve. The pilot who turns aside exposes his full profile to the enemy at close range. At least that's what I've heard. I've never done this before.

I concentrate on flying straight. I clutch the handle of my Lewis gun and carefully hold my finger away from the trigger. The urge to pull out of this suicidal move is almost overwhelming, but if I do, I'm dead for sure. Finally, I slide my finger through the trigger guard and squeeze. At that instant, the other pilot dives beneath me. I see his windshield shatter and a line of holes appear down his fuselage, then he's gone. I twist round to see the Fokker fall into a spin, a stream of dark smoke pouring from his engine.

I don't have time to follow him down because there are three other Fokkers around me. I move the stick, kick the rudder and snap the Parasol round in a tight turn. My engine protests loudly. A Fokker flashes in front of me. Instinctively, my finger tightens on the trigger—but nothing happens. My gun's jammed. I lean forward and hammer the side of the weapon, and as I do, I catch a glimpse of another Fokker coming at me and feel a splash of hot oil as a bullet thuds into my engine. I throw myself back into my seat and wrench the stick over to turn toward the attacker. The move surprises him and he flashes above me, but with a last protesting cough, my engine dies into silence.

That's it. With no power, I can't maneuver. If I go into a spin, I won't be able to get out of it. The Fokkers have me at their mercy. All I can do is dive for home and prolong the process. I turn west and push the nose down, expecting to feel the bullets tearing into my back at any minute. Nothing happens. I twist back to see why. The three Fokkers aren't following me because they are fully engaged in a twirling, twisting dogfight with two Parasols. Already one of the Fokkers is spiraling down in flames.

I ease out of the dive to maintain altitude. I fiddle with the controls and my engine kicks back into life, but it sounds horribly rough. I glance back over my shoulder. One of the Parasols is snaking and weaving, trying to throw off a Fokker clinging to his tail. The last Fokker is already running for home, and the second Parasol is closing in to help his mate. The uneven fight doesn't last long; the Fokker's wings fold and he drops.

The two Parasols catch me easily and fall into formation, one on either side. I look left to see Bowie beaming at me and giving the thumbs-up. I wave back.

I look right and see Mick staring determinedly ahead. I wave, but he doesn't acknowledge me. Still, relief floods through me. I'm alive. I have enough height to make it over the lines, and I'm protected by the two best pilots in the squadron.

I laugh out loud and, even though he can't hear me, shout over at Mick. "Cheer up! We're alive, and we got three Fokkers." As if in reply, Mick's head slumps forward onto his chest and the Parasol's nose lurches into a steep dive.

I twist round to see who's attacking us, but the sky's empty. I look down. Mick's plane has gone into a wild spin. Bowie is following him down, but there's nothing he can do. Mick must have been wounded in the fight and either died or passed out from loss of blood. I can't watch him crash, so I concentrate on getting home.

I'm still over the German lines, so I throw out the two twenty-pound bombs to lighten the plane. The panorama below me has changed in the last hour. Now there are flashes of guns below me. German guns. The ones that our artillery was supposed to have destroyed. Our barrage is still firing, but the shell bursts are over the German reserve trenches, not their front lines. Does that mean the attack's going according to plan?

I risk flying lower as I cross the German front lines. They're badly battered, but there are men in them— ours or theirs? The helmets don't look quite right, and some of the men shoot at me. I curse the sputtering engine that prevents me from maneuvering lower to be sure. I flash over the German wire, which is intact apart from occasional gaps. A few shells are exploding in no-man's-land, but there's no sign of life. All I see are dark hummocks spread through the grass. Most are scattered, but some lie in puzzling straight rows. What does it all mean?

Shells are also exploding over the British trenches, which are packed with soldiers preparing to go over

SOLDIERS EMERGING FROM THE TRENCHES.

the top. I fly over St. John's Road and see the Newfound-landers waiting too. Are Raleigh and Broughton down there? If so, what awaits them?

CHAPTER 17

Tragedy—July 1, 1916

I don't see Bowie again and assume he has resumed his work spotting the infantry advance. I'm able to land without incident, and Wally hurries over to see what happened. "Are you all right?" he asks.

I nod. "Engine's gone, though." As we walk over to the chateau, I tell him about Mick. Wally doesn't say anything. "How's the attack going?" I finally ask.

"As far as I can tell, well. One of the new pilots returned to tell me that he'd seen khaki uniforms in the German reserve trenches outside Beaumont-Hamel. I radioed it in to headquarters."

I get a hollow feeling in the pit of my stomach. "I'm not sure that's right," I say. "I couldn't get low enough to be certain, but I thought I saw Germans in their front line trenches. Their artillery is certainly shelling our trenches, and there are a lot of bodies in no-man's-land, which must be ours. Why would Fritz be in no-man's-land?"

Wally looks thoughtful. "I need more than 'I thought I saw' before I can radio in a report."

"Is the pilot who reported still here?" I ask.

"Yes. That's his Parasol being refueled over there. He must be in the chateau."

We hurry over the grass. As we approach, the pilot comes out the main door.

"What did you see?" I shout at him.

He looks like a startled rabbit.

"When you flew over the lines," I demand. "What did you see?"

"I saw men in the German trenches in front of Beaumont-Hamel."

"Are you certain they were *our* men?" I'm standing in front of him now. He looks nervous.

"Yes," he says, but his eyes don't meet mine.

"What height were you flying at?" My voice is rising and the pilot's shifting from foot to foot.

"Low," he says.

"Five hundred feet?"

"A bit higher," he says quietly.

"A thousand feet?" I'm almost screaming at him.

He says nothing and stares at his boots. I grab him by the lapels and haul him forward until his face is inches from mine.

"A thousand feet?" I yell into his face.

"Higher," he says, his voice barely audible.

I shove him away violently. "You can't recognize uniforms from that height, especially when they're in trenches and covered in mud. Those were German soldiers you saw!"

"You fool," Wally says. "HQ is going to send the Newfoundlanders into no-man's-land to support gains that haven't been made. They'll walk into German machine guns and unbroken wire!"

The boy looks as if he's going to burst into tears, but I don't care. I push him out of the way and run toward his machine, shoving the startled fitter away.

"Start her up," I yell as I scramble into the cockpit.

"What are you going to do?" Wally asks.

"I don't know. Anything I can." The engine kicks into life and I taxi the Parasol to the end of the runway. I glance at my watch—almost 9 a.m. Has it been only two hours since I took off this morning?

I roar down the runway and barely clear the poplars along the road. I don't bother climbing, heading east at treetop height. Men look up and horses buck with fright as I thunder over. There's Beaumont-Hamel, sitting on its ridge with the mine crater in front of it and the smoke and debris from British shells swirling around it. Very gently—I can't afford any mistakes at this altitude—I bank to the right. There's St. John's Road with the trench running beside it. The trench is still packed with soldiers, so the Newfoundlanders haven't attacked yet. My sense of relief fades, though, as I get closer. The men are fitting bayonets onto their rifles.

I zoom along the trench, mere feet above the men's heads. Some look up. An officer—Raleigh?—waves, looks at his watch and places a whistle to his mouth. I scream, "No! Stop!" but it's no use. No one can hear me. All I can do is watch helplessly as the men clamber up the side of the trench.

The communication trenches that should cover them until they reach the front line are so packed with dead and wounded that the Newfoundlanders have to walk over open ground before they even get to no-man's-land. As soon as they stand up, men begin to fall—not dramatically, they just seem to be tired and slump down. The rest lean forward as if walking into a strong wind. There's no one attacking on either side of them and no supporting artillery barrage—just eight hundred Newfoundlanders taking on the whole German army.

German soldiers are climbing onto the lip of their trenches to kneel so that they can get a better aim. Screaming and cursing, I fly back and forth emptying my Lewis gun at them.

The Newfoundlanders have reached the British wire now. There, they bunch together to get through the gaps. They fall in heaps, and those coming behind have to climb over the bodies of their comrades. There are not many left by the time the survivors spread out in no-man's-land, but they keep going. A handful make it to the solitary tree that I nearly hit. A few almost make it to the German wire before they are cut down.

Fifteen minutes after I arrived over St. John's Road, the battlefield is silent. A few figures are trying to crawl back to the safety of their own lines, but most lie still.

I fly along the front one more time, tears flowing freely down my cheeks. The Germans don't even bother to fire at me. Why should they? They've won.

I climb until the tragedy outside Beaumont-Hamel just looks like the rest of the world—up to where I am far from the death and destruction into the clean, cold air where birds soar, oblivious to what goes on below. This is where I want to be. This is why I learned to fly. This is what I thought flying in the war would be like. If only I could stay up here forever, free from the insanity below, but I know I can't. Mick was right—you may not start a war, but once it's begun, you fight to win. What he didn't say was that the war begins to control you. I wipe my tears away and turn the Parasol for home. Wally will be wanting a report.

"Least Mick didn't flame out," Bowie says, slurring his words. He, Wally and I are sitting on the couch in the chateau discussing the day. Other pilots I don't know, and don't want to know, sit elsewhere around the room. We're all exhausted and depressed. Bowie is drunk. He swears viciously under his breath. "Disaster," he snarls.

"They say the French made some progress to the south," Wally counters, but there's no spirit in his voice.

Bowie and I each went up on three more sorties that day, but they were uneventful. The fighting below us petered out in the afternoon, and we were left staring at the sad lumps of khaki scattered across no-man's-land. As far as we could tell, the German front lines were completely unbroken.

"Your friend okay?" Wally asks.

"Alec's fine," I reply. I have just returned from scrounging a ride over to the remnants of the Newfoundland Regiment to find Alec. He's safe, but Raleigh's dead—he didn't even make it to the Newfoundland front line before the bullets found him—and Broughton is missing.

"Only sixty-eight men answered roll call this afternoon. Sixty-eight out of nearly eight hundred."

"It's a catastrophe." Bowie takes another swig of his drink.

"What happens next?" I ask Wally.

He shrugs. "We go on. We've orders to go up tomorrow and assess the situation."

"Assess the situation!" Bowie shouts. "I'll tell you what the situation is—those boys who ain't dead in no-man's-land are back exactly where they started at 7:30 this morning. We don't need to fly to know that."

"But we will," Wally says calmly. "We have to go on. What's the alternative? Surrender?"

Bowie slumps deeper into the couch, his anger spent. "The whole thing's a fiasco," he mumbles into his drink.

"I've got reports to finish," Wally says, standing. "I suggest you two get some sleep."

Bowie grunts, but I stand up and move over to my bunk. Even if I can't sleep, bed is preferable to watching Bowie sink deeper into his alcoholic misery.

I listen to the tent flap mournfully in the breeze. Bowie's right—the day has been a horrible disaster, and I have lost more friends. But I'm alive. It's selfish, but I'm glad I'm not huddled in a damp hole in the wall of a trench or struggling in agony to drag my broken body across no-man's-land to safety. I think back to my first magical flights with Horst, soaring through the blue above the empty prairie, the railway disappearing in both directions. It was wonderful, thrilling—and it was safe.

An odd thought pops into my mind. If a genie suddenly appeared and gave me a choice—tomorrow I could either spend the day in complete security, twisting and turning in the skies above Mortlach, Parkbeg and Moose Jaw, or stay here and go on endless patrols over the horrors of Beaumont-Hamel with Bowie and Wally—what would I do? I know beyond a shadow of a doubt that I would choose here.

Is that normal? I don't know, but this is my life now. Alec, Bowie and Wally are my friends; they're as important to me as my family, living in blissful ignorance back in Saskatchewan. We've shared too much—the thrill of taking off into a dawn sky not knowing what's ahead, the tension of watching for Fokkers diving out of the sun, the chaotic excitement of a swirling dogfight, the fear of knowing Fritz is on your tail, the relief at still being alive at the end of the day. Could I live without that? It's not what I wanted or expected when I came to this war, but it's what I am, and I cannot deny that.

Nearby, I hear Bowie snoring loudly on the couch. "Good night, Bowie," I say into the darkness, before I drift off into a surprisingly peaceful sleep.

Author's Note

While the main characters in *Wings of War* are fictional, the historical background is accurate. For example, the planes that Edward learns and fights in are the actual machines of that time, and Immelmann and his turn are real. Uncle Horst's Berthas are fictional, although the early years of the twentieth century were a time when enthusiasts could, and did, build planes in their barns. There are even suggestions that some managed powered flight before the Wright Brothers in 1903. As early as 1890, there are stories of a French inventor, Clement Ader, flying fifty metres in a bat-like plane

powered by a steam engine. Most books on flying in
WWI concentrate on 1917/18 and the well-known flyers
like Billy Bishop and the Red Baron. I was intrigued by
the earlier years, when flying was still a solitary pursuit
and the pilots wrestled with a changing technology
where a small advance, such as inventing a machine
gun that could fire straight ahead through a plane's
propeller, could tilt the balance wildly in favour of one
side or the other and mean life or death for a pilot.
When WWI began, few people saw airplanes as anything other than a novelty that might have a minor use
in helping the cavalry spot enemy movements. The
idea that planes could be so big and fast that hundreds
of them together could destroy a city was science fic-
tion. In 1915, solitary planes, usually slow two-seaters,
would go up and examine and photograph the enemy
trenches. If they were protected at all, it was by a single
scout plane, like Edward's Morane Parasol. If fights
broke out, they would be between individual flyers. By
1916, planes flew in groups of two or three and the idea
of swirling, chaotic dogfights had taken hold. Planes
were also being used for other purposes than simple
reconnaissance. By the Battle of the Somme, they were
communicating with troops, supporting them with
machine-gun fire and even carrying small bombs to
drop on concentrations of the enemy. This was still a

far cry from the deadly Flying Circus of the Red Baron and the sleek, fast fighters and huge bombers of 1918, but it was an important step towards it. There are many books on flying in WWI, but the best that deals with the time in which *Wings of War* is set is *Sagittarius Rising*, the memoir of Cecil Arthur Lewis's experiences in WWI. Lewis flew Morane Parasols and won the Military Cross over the Battle of the Somme in 1916. He actually did see huge shells passing his plane during the pre-battle bombardment. The movie *Aces High* is partly based on Lewis's memoirs and has some wonderful dogfight scenes.

Glossary

Ace—In the Royal Flying Corps, a pilot who has shot down five enemy planes.

Amiens—A town in northern France, far enough from the front lines that it was a safe place to recover from a wound.

Archie—Pilot slang for anti-aircraft fire from the ground.

Beaumont-Hamel—A town that was fortified by the Germans and formed part of the front lines that were attacked by the Newfoundland Regiment on July 1, 1916. Beaumont-Hamel was not captured until November 1916.

Berlin, Ontario—The name of Kitchener, Ontario, before it was changed in 1916.

Biplane—A plane with two layers of wings, most often one above and one below the pilot. This was the most common type of plane in the First World War.

Louis Blériot—The first pilot to fly over the English Channel, in 1909. For many years after his feat, he sold versions of his monoplane all over the world.

Camouflet—A small mine that was exploded to destroy enemy tunnels rather than trenches.

Chateau—A large French country house.

Dogfight—A battle between opposing planes in midair. So called because when dogs fight, they form a chaotic, churning mass.

Dressing station—The first place a wounded soldier could receive treatment behind the front line trenches.

From there they would be sent farther away to hospitals or even over to England.

Duckboard—Slatted wooden boards that were laid on the floor of trenches to make walking easier.

Archduke Franz Ferdinand—The heir to the throne of the Austro-Hungarian Empire. His assassination in Sarajevo in 1914 triggered the outbreak of the First World War.

Fire step—Trenches had to be deep enough so that soldiers could walk along them without their heads sticking above the parapet. The fire step was provided so they could step up to see or shoot out into no-man's-land.

Fitter—A mechanic whose job was to service fighter planes between sorties.

Fritz—A slang term for a German soldier or pilot.

Front lines—The trenches closest to the enemy.

Gas curtain—A heavy canvas curtain hung over the entrance to a dugout to prevent poison gas getting in.

Hangar—A large shed for storing planes.

Hun—A slang term for a German.

Max Immelmann—The first German ace and inventor of the Immelmann turn. The Pour le Mérite medal was nicknamed the Blue Max in his honor.

Immelmann turn—A manoeuver designed by Immelmann to gain an advantage on an enemy in a dogfight.

Lewis gun—A British machine gun with a drum of ammunition that clipped onto the top. It was light and simple enough to be mounted on early fighter planes.

Monoplane—A plane with only one layer of wings. The wings could be above the pilot or extending out from the side of the plane.

Over the top—Slang term for climbing out of the front-line trench to attack the enemy.

Pour le Mérite—The highest order of merit awarded by the Kingdom of Prussia (and Germany after 1870). Many famous German flyers, including Max Immelmann and the Red Baron, were awarded the

Pour le Mérite in the First World War. The last one was given in 1918.

Royal Flying Corps—The British air force in the First World War. It became the Royal Air Force in 1918. Canada did not have its own air force until the Royal Flying Corps Canada was formed in 1917.

Sortie—A flying mission to attack the enemy or carry out reconnaissance.

Stand-to—At dawn, the most common time for an attack, the soldiers had to stand to on the fire step to be prepared.

Triplane—A plane with three layers of wings. Two famous aces, Canada's Raymond Collishaw and Germany's Red Baron, flew these types of planes.

U-boat—A German submarine. From the German *Unterseeboot*, meaning "undersea boat."

Verdun—A French town and the site of one of the biggest battles in the First World War. The battle lasted from February to December 1916.

Kaiser Wilhelm II—King of Prussia and Emperor of Germany from 1888 to 1918.

Wire—Barbed wire that was run along in front of trenches to prevent attackers from getting close.